When Zoe meets the incredibly handsome and charismatic Michael, she has sworn off men for at least six months following another disastrous relationship. Michael is also licking his wounds after losing his long-term girlfriend to his scheming brother. But one date is all it takes for them both to realise they can't fight the chemistry that burns between them.

Despite his charms, Zoe soon begins to wonder if Michael is hiding something from her—he is, and the truth leads her on a romantic adventure filled with glamorous locations, family secrets and almost unbearable passion.

Michael isn't the humble hotel worker he initially claims to be—he's the multi-millionaire CEO of an international hotel chain, and someone is trying to sabotage his company. Meanwhile his obnoxious younger brother seems intent on derailing any chance Zoe and Michael have of a happy ending.

Can their blossoming love survive the rollercoaster ride that is Michael's life—a world of love, vengeance and lies?

Love, Vengeance, and Lies

ISBN: 978-1-4874-3124-2
Cover art by Martine Jardin

Published by eXtasy Books Inc or
Devine Destinies, an imprint of eXtasy Books Inc

Look for us online at:
www.eXtasybooks.com or www.devinedestinies.com

Love, Vengeance, and Lies

By

M.S. Batham

Chapter One

Zoe wondered how she hadn't seen it coming. Doug had been acting weird all week—working late at the office, remembering he'd made plans with friends on the nights he was supposed to be meeting her, and cutting short pretty much every telephone conversation they'd had, making some lame excuse as to why he needed to go. When he'd called that morning to suggest they go for dinner, Zoe had been happy at first. Maybe he was coming out the other end of whatever mood he'd been in. But sitting opposite him now, in the nondescript Bistro in Soho, Zoe was feeling anything but happy. Despite all the warnings, she felt shell-shocked.

"Zoe? Are you okay?" Doug leaned forward, his brown eyes actually showing a trace of concern. He tried to take her hand, but she snatched it free.

"Am I okay?" she asked, fixing her gaze on him. She tried not to think about how handsome he looked, with that firm jawline and swept back blond hair. Those looks had drawn her in too many times. Those eyes had persuaded her to take him back on more than one occasion.

"Am I okay?" she repeated, louder this time, causing Doug to glance around the restaurant, obviously embarrassed and worried she was going to cause a scene.

"Please don't get upset," he said, which annoyed her even more. Now she knew why he'd bought her here rather than one of their regular haunts. He didn't want to be shown up in a restaurant he might go back to.

"You've just told me you're having an affair with some

bimbo you work with and you want me to calm down!"

"It's not really an affair, Zoe. You and I aren't married. We don't even live together. I've just met someone else and I want to see where it goes."

Zoe was feeling hot. Hot and furious. This stupid man had messed her around one too many times. She stood, picking up an almost full bottle of red wine from the table.

"Well, let's see where this goes," she said, tipping the bottle up so that red liquid sloshed onto the edge of the table nearest Doug, splashing across his lap, ruining his Saville Row suit trousers.

"Jesus!" Doug leaped to his feet, arms spread in an expression of dismay and disbelief. Oher diners had now stopped speaking and were turning to stare, but Zoe didn't care. She'd had enough. He deserved to be embarrassed and humiliated.

She slammed the now empty bottle back on the table, grabbed her coat from the back of her chair, and headed for the door, sidestepping two waiters rushing toward the scene of the crime.

Don't look back!

She reached the door and remembered to pull rather than push it open. The cool air hit her and was very welcome. She stood taking deep breaths for a moment, then still without looking back, headed toward the nearest Underground station.

She managed to contain her emotions until she reached her apartment in Islington, but as soon as the door had closed behind her, she burst into tears. It wasn't sadness over losing Doug that was making her cry, it was frustration and anger at herself for ever having taken him back. He'd always been flaky and scared of commitment, but every time he asked her to forgive him, she had, always hoping this time he'd change. But he never did, and now he'd committed the ultimate act of disloyalty and slept with someone else. Maybe this wasn't the first time. Perhaps all those other occasions when he'd said they should have a break, there'd been another woman waiting in the wings, but he hadn't bothered to mention them.

Was there something special about this latest assignation?

Who cares! This time he really is history!

Zoe surveyed her apartment. She was pretty lucky. She was living in an affluent part of London, a nice one-bed conversion in a striking period property, and she had regular freelance work as a content writer for a very successful fashion retailer's website. A lot of women of her age, thirty-one, would kill for a life like hers. She didn't need a man in her life. She had everything she required, and she'd earned it all herself. Doug could take his City job and his bespoke suits and . . .

Zoe wandered over to the large ornate mirror above the fireplace in her living room.

Am I really going to do the self-analysis in the mirror?

Yes, she was going to, but it was all positive. She looked great. Despite being slightly puffy and bloodshot, her eyes were a stunning green, her narrow nose a perfect contrast to her full lips, and her brunette hair was lush and full, falling in natural waves to her shoulders. She gave her locks a defiant flick, turned, and strode to the sofa, sitting heavily and looking for her cigarettes.

I gave up a year ago, remember.

She began to cry again. How could she have wasted three years of her life on that man?

She wiped her eyes on the back of her hand and sniffed.

"New start!" she announced aloud—then, worried her neighbours downstairs might think she was going mad, she continued the pep talk in her head.

Tomorrow is Saturday. I am going to wake up and do something I've never done before – something for me. It doesn't have to be anything huge, just something different. Tomorrow is my day.

She glanced at her watch. It was only ten o'clock, but she was tired and wanted to wake up feeling fresh and positive.

Tomorrow was going to be the first day of the rest of her life.

It was pouring with rain. Zoe had flung open the curtains of her bedroom window at 8 AM ready to embrace her new day and been faced with a dismal autumn scene. Spears of rain clattered against the window, and the road below was like a river. She'd heard the rain before seeing it, of course, but she'd tried to remain positive. Now that she saw the full ferocity of the weather, her heart sank. Maybe this was a sign of what she could expect from the rest of her life.

Don't be negative! Coffee now!

Obeying her inner voice, Zoe headed to the kitchen and began to make a cafetiere of coffee. She'd take her time getting dressed and then decide what to do. If it continued to pour with rain, she could either catch a taxi somewhere—an art gallery maybe, she hadn't visited an art gallery on her own for years—or she would plan a weekend away somewhere. Perhaps a trip to the coast, Cornwall or Devon. She glanced at the nearest window as hail began to pound the glass. Or maybe she would go abroad where the weather was less unpredictable.

The thought of travelling abroad on her own frightened her, but most of her close friends were now married with kids and not likely to get a pass to come away with her. She could always ask a couple of them to see what they thought. There was Rachael who was single, but Zoe wasn't sure she could cope with a whole week with Rachael. Or she could just bite the bullet and go somewhere on her own. Not just for a weekend, but for a week. Lie by a pool and read loads of books while sipping cocktails, or join an organised hike along a mountain trail. No, cocktails and books by a pool were more her thing. Leaving her comfort zone was one thing, but she didn't have to fling herself out headfirst with no parachute.

By the time she was dressed—she'd chosen an emerald green jump suit and a wide leather belt, as it felt like an outfit that said action—Zoe was feeling upbeat again and ready to do something impulsive. But as she stood at the counter that separated the kitchen from the living area, laptop open in front of her, she had second thoughts. Did she really want to go on holiday alone? Wouldn't she get bored of her own company after a day? Also, she'd had a fairly traumatic few days. Maybe she should start small and just go to an art gallery and then somewhere for lunch. When she got home, she could pour herself a glass of wine and think about her next step toward a more fulfilling life free of men.

It had stopped raining, and the day was actually looking quite bright. She resolved to opt for plan B, and grabbing a denim jacket from a hook next to the front door, she headed out. Today wouldn't be a massive adventure, but it would be a start.

Zoe had held a romantic notion that she could spend several hours at the Tate Modern, taking time to admire or criticise each piece, before wandering to a café or restaurant on the South Bank for a bite to eat. But after forty minutes, she had already walked through every free gallery, with very little catching her interest, and was now pondering whether she should pay to get into the visiting exhibition. It was a collection by a female Japanese artist who, judging from the video playing above the gallery entrance, liked dots. A lot.

"Are you wondering if it's worth it, too?" asked someone beside her.

Zoe turned to see who the deep but soft voice belonged to.

"Yes," she replied, quickly taking in the chiseled profile, the collar-length almost black, curly hair. "I don't know this artist."

"She's very inventive," said the man, who she guessed was around thirty-five years old. As he spoke, he turned from the video screen to look directly at Zoe. He had beautiful dark-blue eyes. Zoe had never seen eyes quite like them. His skin was faintly tanned, his mouth was full, and when he smiled, she saw that his teeth were a healthy white. He wore a t-shirt with something written on it, but the slogan was obscured by a leather jacket. She glanced down and saw that he was also wearing jeans with a hole in one knee and a pair of well-worn trainers. Not her usual type.

Maybe I need to go for a different type.

What was she thinking? She didn't want to go for any type. She hadn't even been single for a day yet, and she was already sizing up strange men in art galleries.

"I think I'll give it a miss," said Zoe. "I'm feeling hungry anyway."

"Me too," said the man.

Zoe turned and walked toward the escalator that would take her down to the Turbine Hall, as the ground floor of the gallery was known.

Suddenly the man was beside her again.

"Would you like to join me for lunch?"

"What?" Zoe was too shocked to respond politely.

The man laughed. "Sorry, I didn't mean to freak you out. I'm not a weirdo. I just thought if we were both having a day out alone, we could maybe chat for a while over some nice food."

Zoe glanced again at his casual attire and wondered if what he was really asking was if she would buy him lunch.

"My treat," he said, as if reading her mind.

"I . . ." Zoe floundered for something to say.

The man took a step away from her. "I'm sorry, I've stressed you out. I really didn't mean to. I don't normally ask strangers to lunch, but it's been one of those weeks and I promised myself I'd act on impulse today. I'll leave you to enjoy your day."

He turned and walked back toward the gallery. Zoe watched him go, admiring his broad shoulders and long, muscular legs clad in tight black denim.

Why not!

"Wait!" she called and he turned back, looking confused.

She hurried over to him. "Yes," she said, as she drew close. "I would like to go to lunch. But I'm not looking for any romance right now. I just split up from someone, and I want to enjoy some time being single."

The man laughed, his cheeks creasing into dimples. "That's fine. I really was just suggesting lunch and a chat. We seem to be in the same boat today."

"Well, let's row it to a restaurant." Zoe made sure she didn't giggle at her own attempt at a joke.

His name was Michael Braden and he worked in a hotel. How refreshing was that? Not some city boy or high-risk financier, a down-to-earth guy who worked in a hotel.

Zoe asked him what he'd meant about being in the same boat as her, and as they sat outside the pub just a short walk from the Tate Modern with a view across the Thames, he told her.

"I was seeing someone up until a couple of weeks ago," he said, zipping up his jacket against the breeze blowing up from the river. "A woman called Lucy. I was really into her. I'd actually bought a ring. I was going to pop the question. Then two days before I'd planned to take her somewhere romantic and ask her to marry me, she told me she was in love with someone else."

Zoe pulled a suitably sympathetic expression. "That's awful."

"My younger brother," said Michael.

"What? No!"

Michael nodded. "Yes, my dear sweet brother, Samuel. Stole my girl from me, and she was very happy to be stolen. She's already moved in with him—she refused to move in with me until we were at least engaged. But she and Samuel are nice and cosy in his penthouse in Chelsea."

"Penthouse?" Zoe tried not to sound impressed.

"Yes, he's quite well off," said Michael. "But what about you? What's your story?"

Zoe briefly related her recent experience with Doug without making herself look too much of a victim. Not that it mattered what Michael thought of her really, as they wouldn't see each other again after this lunch by the Thames. As far as she was concerned, and she thought he felt the same, this was a one-off impulsive adventure for two recently single people.

Nothing more than that, Zoe told herself, trying not to stare too long into his beautiful eyes. She was also drawn to his quiet confidence. Despite his casual attire he sat upright, broad shoulders back, chin up. He had the stance of a powerful man, despite being just a normal guy.

"What an idiot," said Michael, in response to her story.

"I could say the same about Lucy," said Zoe, as the waitress arrived with their food orders.

They'd both ordered club sandwiches and fries. Simple, non-pretentious food in a basic pub. If this had been lunch with Doug, they would have been in some pretentious eatery, with about six waiters fussing round them. Zoe preferred the current scenario She felt she could breathe and just enjoy the conversation.

"Go on, then," said Michael as the waitress left.

"What?" Zoe looked from her food to Michael.

"Say the same about Lucy."

Zoe laughed. "Lucy was a complete and utter idiot," she said.

They chatted easily, although Zoe couldn't help but feel she was doing most of the talking. But it was nice to have a man listen and show an interest in what she had to say, especially a man as handsome as Michael. Zoe wondered what his brother Samuel looked like. Surely it must have been his money that tempted Lucy away from Michael. Again she was struck by his easy charisma. It radiated from him. It was almost overwhelming that a guy so ordinary in many ways had such presence.

Will you stop it! You are a proud single woman and happy to stay that way for at least a few months!

"Do you fancy a walk along the river?" asked Michael as they finished their meals.

"I need to head back to Waterloo Station anyway," she replied, dabbing her mouth with a napkin. "So you can walk with me if you want."

Michael ushered the waitress over and handed her several notes. "Keep the change," he told her, and the waitress looked shocked. "It's fine," Michael added.

The waitress wandered back inside looking slightly stunned.

Zoe watched her walk away. "How much did you tip her?"

"Only a few quid," said Michael. "They probably don't get many tips in here. Come on, we need to walk fast, its clouding over again."

As they walked along the Thames, Zoe pondered how relaxed she felt with this almost total stranger. They continued to talk until they reached London Bridge, where Zoe needed to turn left away from the river toward the station.

They both stopped and turned to face each other.

"Thank you for lunch," she said, feeling awkward for the first time since their meeting.

"Thanks for getting into my boat," said Michael with a wink.

Zoe smiled. "Our boat, I think you'll find."

They hesitated, Zoe wanted to say more, and from his expression, Michael did, too. But they had agreed just lunch and nothing more. Zoe decided to take the lead, however hard it was to just walk away from him.

"Bye, then." She pecked him on the cheek and turned

quickly before he could see her blush. She felt a little woozy as she headed past the National Theatre toward the road that led to Waterloo Station.

But I didn't even have a glass of wine with lunch.

Zoe risked a glance back over her shoulder and saw Michael standing in the same spot, watching her. He waved and smiled then turned and walked to the wall next to the river, resting his hands on top of it and gazing toward the far bank.

Zoe was so tempted to run back and give him her phone number, but that wasn't what today was about. Today was about her celebrating herself and enjoying the single life. She'd go home now and book that week abroad.

But as she continued to walk away from the river and from Michael, her heart felt heavy.

Chapter Two

Zoe couldn't stop thinking about Michael. All week she'd been distracted, finding it hard to focus on her work because his face would suddenly pop into her mind. It didn't help that she worked from home, so there was no-one else around to help her stop moping and get on with writing the next piece of content.

It was now Friday, and still she was thinking about Michael, his dark-blue eyes and those sensual lips, his deep but gentle voice and those dimples when he grinned. And that powerful presence, how he commanded attention without seeming to try.

So much for not thinking about men.

On the plus side, she'd barely given Doug a second thought. Even the idea of him with another woman didn't bother her. It was as if meeting Michael had completely eclipsed any feeling she'd had for Doug. Mind you, Doug had done a good job of destroying those feelings himself.

Zoe closed her laptop and leaned back in her chair. It was five o'clock on a Friday evening – she might as well stop work for the day. It wasn't as if she was being very productive, and her next deadline wasn't until Wednesday.

Her mobile phone rang, and for a moment she had the stupid idea that it would be Michael, but how could it be? They hadn't even swapped numbers. She picked the phone up from her desk and saw the caller's name on the screen. Doug.

Seriously?

She hesitated before accepting the call.

"Babe?" Even hearing him say this one word irritated her.

"What is it, Doug? I'm working."

"I just wanted to hear your voice." He actually sounded emotional.

"Why?"

There was a pause while Doug obviously adjusted to her hostile tone.

"I miss you," he said finally, and his voice cracked.

"Are you for real? A week ago you dumped me in a restaurant because you wanted to see where things would go with another woman."

"I made a mistake."

"You mean she got tired of you already?"

Another pause followed.

"Can we meet?" he asked eventually.

"No," said Zoe.

"Really?"

"Absolutely not."

"Is there someone else?" Now he sounded desperate.

"That's none of your business, Doug. Please don't call me again."

And she ended the call. She took a deep breath and waited to feel some kind of emotion, but she just felt glad to be rid of him. Rid of his lies and his annoying apologies.

Even the memory of his perfectly pressed suits and expensive cologne irritated her now, and she had once been so attracted to his well-groomed image and loved the outline of his toned physique in a tight-fitting white shirt.

Careful!

But it was fine. Even imagining him naked and aroused did nothing for her.

Suddenly an image of Michael lying naked on a bed of white sheets popped into her head. Obviously, she had to imagine what his body would look like, but she had seen enough to know he was slim but toned, broad-shouldered and narrow-waisted. He stared up at her with his stunning eyes and whispered *come and join me,* forming each word with those full lips. And even in her imagination, his softly spoken words carried the force of a command.

Zoe stood up and opened the nearest window. She felt very warm all of a sudden.

It was still a bright autumn day, although it would be dark in in hour or so. Zoe decided to get out, breathe some fresh air and clear her head of thoughts of Michael Braden.

As she stepped out onto the pavement and turned to pull the front door closed, her phoned beeped. She almost ignored it but decided to check in case it was a message from someone at work. It was only five-thirty, and officially she was on duty until six o'clock. She squinted down at the phone screen, which was hard to see because of the low sun.

It was a Facebook direct message that had come through. She clicked on the appropriate app icon, expecting some annoying *pass this on* group message. But the face that grinned out at her next to the three lines of type was Michael's. She shielded the screen with her other hand to get a better look. It was definitely him. Michael Braden. The message was straight to the point.

There are a lot of people called Zoe living in London. But I found you! Hope that's okay. Would you like to meet up again?

Zoe was grinning and resisting the urge to punch the air. He'd actually searched through every Zoe in London on Facebook to find her. That showed commitment.

Or obsessive behaviour.

She clicked through to his Facebook profile. It appeared he'd set it up purely to get in touch with her, as it contained the absolute minimum of information and he had no friends.

Obsessive and friendless.

"Oh shut up!" Zoe said aloud, attracting a strange look from an elderly man passing close by. "Not you," she added hastily.

So, it was crunch time. Did she respond and say yes to meeting up? Or stick to her guns and avoid dating anyone for at least a few months, enjoy some quality me time, get to know herself again and rediscover what really mattered?

She responded to Michael's message.

I can't believe you went to so much effort. I'd love to meet up. When are you free?

Zoe let herself back into the house and climbed the stairs to her second-floor apartment She had gone off the idea of taking a walk. She needed to sit down and process what had just happened.

She poured herself a glass of white wine and sat on the sofa, re-reading Michael's message. As she stared at the screen a new text appeared.

How about tonight? Or does that sound too keen? Or presumptuous?

It was actually refreshing. No game playing. No trying to play it cool. Although having scrolled through hundreds of Facebook members called Zoe from London, it was a bit late for Michael to try playing it cool.

But what should she do? Firstly, did she want to get involved with someone new so soon after Doug? And secondly, did she want Michael knowing she had no plans on a Friday night, or was prepared to drop any she did have to see him?

He's not playing games, so why should I?

She typed her reply.

I was meant to be seeing some friends, but they had to cancel so I am free tonight. Fancy grabbing a bite to eat?

It didn't do any harm so lie just a little bit. He responded immediately.

Brilliant! Yes, dinner sounds good. I can book us a table somewhere. Italian okay for you? I know a nice place in Fitzrovia, just off Goodge Street. I can send you the booking details. Eight o'clock okay for you? You can say no to any of the above, obviously.

Zoe smiled. It made a nice change from Doug dictating

where they went on their dates. Normally she would just receive a forwarded booking confirmation email from him. He always said she could choose somewhere else if she wanted, but on the rare occasion she did, he would pick faults with everything from the slow service to the temperature of the wine. In the end she had just let him have his way. But she wouldn't fall into that trap again.

She decided to test just how flexible Michael was with her reply.

Do you mind if we don't do Italian? I really fancy Thai and there's a great restaurant near to Angel tube station. I can book it for eight if that works for you and meet you outside the tube.

She waited. A minute passed. Maybe he wasn't happy not to be charge after all. If that was the case, she was better off knowing now, rather than getting involved with another control freak.

Finally, he responded.

Sounds good. I'll see you at the station at eight. Looking forward to it. Glad I didn't scare you off.

Zoe grinned, then headed for the bathroom. She needed to shower and choose a first-date outfit.

Don't call it a date!

Oh, who was she kidding? Of course it was a date.

As she made the ten-minute walk from her home to Angel Underground station, Zoe wondered if Michael would be on time. She felt like a twenty-year-old again, meeting a boy outside a tube station rather than getting picked up in a cab and whisked to a restaurant. She liked it, although the intensity of the feelings she already felt for Michael scared her a little. No doubt after a proper date, she would start to see his faults and he'd no longer be the fantasy lover she was turning him into.

As she drew close to the station, she saw him waiting by the exit. He was gazing into space, dark hair falling across his forehead. He was wearing a pair of faded blue jeans, but these didn't appear to have any holes in them, and the leather jacket had been replaced by a knee-length grey overcoat. Zoe's stomach did a small somersault at the sight of him. He stood out from the crowds, his incredible charisma like an aura around him. When he spotted her approaching through the crowd of Friday night revellers and grinned his delicious grin, her heart flipped, too.

I need to calm down!

"Hi!" he greeted, walking toward her with his arms spread wide. He pulled her in for a hug and planted a kiss on her cheek.

Don't blush! Don't blush!

She blushed.

"The restaurant is just up here," Zoe turned away from him to hide her red face and started walking back the way she had come. "It's great food and not that expensive."

"Sounds good," said Michael, walking beside her. "So you weren't freaked out that I tracked you down? I was worried you'd think I was some kind of stalker."

Zoe laughed. "Not at all. It was good to hear from you. I was starting to regret not swapping numbers. I mean, just because we're not looking for a relationship, doesn't mean we can't meet up with people of the opposite sex, right?"

"Er . . . right."

"Here we are." Zoe, pushed open the door to an unassuming Thai restaurant and led the way in.

They were greeted warmly by a pretty young waitress and shown to a table at the back of the restaurant. It was separated from the next table by a large potted plant, which meant they'd have some privacy, at least.

"So, any word from your ex?" asked Michael, once they had sat down.

"He called today actually and asked me to go back to him," replied Zoe, picking up her menu and scanning the starters.

"And?"

She peered round the large menu. "I told him where to go."

"Oh good," said Michael. "I mean good for you."

The waitress returned to take their drinks order. Michael ordered a bottled beer, Zoe a gin and tonic. She wondered if they would share a bottle of wine with their food. She really fancied a chilled white wine.

"What about Lucy, any word from her?" asked Zoe.

"Well, I had to see her the other day at a family get-together. My dad was seventy on Wednesday and wanted everyone to meet up at a restaurant in Chiswick. They have a small apartment there. Samuel turned up with Lucy on his arm, bold as brass. My poor parents looked very uncomfortable. I thought I would feel more than I did, to be honest. I just looked at her and felt irritated by her presence more than anything. Not jealous or upset."

"That's how I feel about Doug. Everything he said earlier just irritated me. And even when I think about him, I just feel resentful that I wasted so much time on him."

"You're doing well considering it only ended a week ago. At least I've had a few weeks to get used to the situation."

"I might not be doing so well if Doug was dating my sister," said Zoe.

Michael nodded. "I must admit, I do have a problem with Samuel. I could barely bring myself to speak to him on Wednesday. I only did because I didn't want to upset my parents. At the end of the day, what he did was despicable. You don't steal your brother's girlfriend, however much you claim to be in love with her."

Zoe saw another side to Michael as he talked about his brother. His voice grew sharper and his dark eyes blazed. The image of him splayed naked on the bed jumped back into her head, except this time he wasn't asking her gently to join him, he was pulling her down on top of him, kissing her forcefully, his hand sliding down her back, resting on her buttocks.

"Zoe?"

"Sorry?" Zoe snapped back to reality.

Michael looked at her quizzically. "I just asked if you knew what you were going to order."

"Oh, I haven't even thought about it," she replied, refocusing her attention on the menu.

Zoe soon relaxed into the evening. She managed to stop fantasizing about Michael and just chat to him like she'd done the day they'd met. She needed to just chill and enjoy this for what it was—two newly single people enjoying each other's company.

He tracked me down on Facebook without even knowing my surname!

As they finished their after-dinner coffees, Zoe realised that, once again, she had done most of the talking. Michael asked a lot of questions, and often when she asked him something about himself, he would just answer with a few words and then turn the conversation back round to her. She wasn't even sure where he lived. He'd just replied north west London when she'd asked him.

I need to stop being paranoid. I'm just not used to a man who is more interested in me than himself.

It was true, that after three years with Doug, she had got used to the man doing most of the talking.

As they stood to leave, Michael placed a hand on the small of her back and said, "After you."

It was a tiny gesture, and the physical contact was fleeting, but warmth still spread through Zoe's body, creeping up her neck to her face. She was glad she was heading toward to door with her back to him. She couldn't remember the last time someone had made her blush like this.

She noticed how politely Michael thanked all the staff as they left. Doug would never have bothered doing that.

As she neared the door, a young couple stepped into the

restaurant. The man, who was aged around twenty, smiled, and for a moment Zoe thought she must know him. Then she realised he was looking at Michael.

"Hello, Mr. Britton," the young guy said, still beaming.

Behind her Michael mumbled a response. The man looked confused as she and Michael slid past him and his girlfriend and out of the door.

Zoe glance back and saw the guy watching them and saying something to his girlfriend. He looked upset. Michael gave him a wave and a smile, which seemed to at least partly satisfy him.

"Who was that?" asked Zoe. "And why did he call you Mr. Britton?"

"No idea," said Michael. "I guess I must look like someone he knows."

"But you just waved to him."

"I felt bad. He seemed so happy to see me."

Zoe felt the familiar tug of anxiety that she always experienced when she thought someone wasn't being straight with her. But she let the subject drop.

"Well, thanks for a lovely evening," she said.

"Is it over?" asked Michael, taking her hand and staring into her eyes.

If it hadn't been for the new sense of unease she was feeling, she would have been tempted to invite him back to hers and discover how accurate her fantasy version of him was. But something about the encounter with the young man had spoiled the evening for Zoe and she just wanted to get home—alone. She pulled her hand free and gave Michael a chaste kiss on the cheek. "I need my bed. It's been a long week. Thanks again."

And she walked away. For the second time in a week she was turning her back on Michael and heading home, but tonight her heart felt heavy for a different reason. She was wondering if Michael Braden, if that was really his name, was someone she could trust after all.

When she arrived home she immediately went to her desk and opened her laptop.

She clicked on the Internet browser icon and entered Michael Britain into the search field.

A message appeared above the various page links. *Do you mean Michael Britton?* Zoe shrugged and searched that name instead.

The third link down showed a row of images. She clicked on the first one, but even from the thumbnail, she could tell it was Michael. It was a corporate head and shoulders shot, but he was smiling his glowing grin. The caption on the image read *Michael Britton, CEO of the Britton Hotel Group.*

Zoe repeated the name to herself. It was familiar. She'd stayed in a Britton Hotel in France with Doug. It had been a huge, glittering place, one of the most luxurious hotels she had ever stayed in in fact. It was hard to connect the Michael she knew, or thought she knew, with such a haven of wealth.

She pictured Michael in his ripped jeans and leather jacket and remembered his avoidance of questions about his work. Why had he lied about who he was?

She clicked on another link. This one took her to a hotel trade website, where Michael was pictured with a very attractive blonde woman leaving an event. The caption for this image read *Millionaire Hotelier Michael Britton and girlfriend Lucy Armitage leaving the International Hotel Awards.*

She slammed the laptop closed and sat back with a heavy sigh. So the handsome, unpretentious Michael Braden was actually the super-rich and apparently deceitful Michael Britton.

Why did he lie?

And why had she let herself be taken in by another man so soon after Doug? So much for her new start.

Her phone beeped. It was a text message from Michael—

they'd swapped numbers over dinner.

You okay? You seemed a bit upset when you said goodbye.

She felt a wave of anger, frustration and disappointment. Having calmed herself, she replied.

No, Michael Britton, I am not okay. I don't like liars. Please don't contact me again.

She hesitated. Did she really want to end this? Shouldn't she at least give him a chance to explain?

That's what the old me would have done.

The inner voice made the decision for her and she pressed send. "Goodbye Michael," she whispered.

Chapter Three

Zoe had a restless night plagued with dreams involving both Michael and Doug. In one, she and Michael had been making love. He was on top of her and inside her, his intense eyes staring into hers. It had felt incredible and so real. But reality had pierced through the dream fabric and she had remembered his deception.

"Why did you lie, Michael?" she'd asked, as he continued to make love to her, his black hair slick with sweat. But then it wasn't Michael looking down at her, it was Doug, square-jawed, muscular Doug, and he felt big inside her, just as he had in reality. She knew she shouldn't be enjoying it, but she was. But when he smiled and whispered, "I love you, Babe," Zoe had remembered why she hated him, and she'd forced herself to wake up.

Now she was lying in tangled sweat-drenched sheets feeling angry with herself for having fantasies about two men who had treated her like dirt. Doug, she knew, was in the past. Now that the dream was over, she had no interest in him sexually. But the memory of Michael, or the dream version of Michael, making love to her as he held her gaze with those penetrating blue eyes was still arousing her. She wanted to experience that feeling for real, but that would mean inviting another lying man into her life, and she just couldn't justify that.

She made herself a large mug of coffee and got back into bed. It was nine o'clock, so she wasn't being too lazy. It was the weekend, after all. She glanced at her phone on the bedside table, picked it up and saw that the screen was dark. Now she remembered turning it off last night so that she wouldn't be tempted to answer any calls or texts from Michael.

Why would he bother chasing after me? He's a filthy rich hotelier.

When she switched the phone back on, it rang almost immediately. It was the voice mail service. It was a message from Michael, asking her to call him to let him explain.

"I know it looks bad," he said, "but I was going to open up to you about everything. I just need to be careful."

She placed the phone back on the bedside table and continued to sip her coffee. If he rang again maybe she'd pick up and give him a chance to explain. It would give her closure if nothing else.

She was about to go and make a second coffee when the phone rang. She snatched it up. It was Michael.

After a short hesitation, she accepted the call. "Yes?"

"Zoe, please listen to me before you hang up."

"Why would I hang up? I could have just ignored the call."

"True. I just want a chance to explain."

"I'm listening."

"Well, as you now know, I am Michael Britton, and my family owns a small chain of hotels across the world."

"Good for you."

"In the past I've had too many women throw themselves at me because they want the money and the lifestyle. So, when I meet someone new, someone outside my social circle who doesn't know who I am, I always introduce myself as Michael Braden."

"You lied about everything," said Zoe.

"I didn't actually lie. I said I worked in a hotel, which technically I do. I just also happen to own it, or ten of them. Well, my family does. And I never lied when I answered your questions, I just avoided telling you anything that would make it obvious I came from money. I just wanted a normal date with a normal woman."

"So, I was a bit of a social experiment?"

"No!" he insisted.

"Is that why you spoke to me at the gallery? Did you think, *she looks really ordinary and normal. Let's see how going on a date with someone like that feels?* Did you actually go to the gallery dressed so casually to ensnare some gullible fool like me?"

"No, I thought, she's gorgeous, I'd like to take her to lunch. And then after lunch I thought, I really like this woman and I'd love to see her again, but we agreed this was a one-off. And then I thought . . ."

"Okay, I get the picture," said Zoe.

"The truth is, Zoe, I don't like the little rich girls who inhabit my social circle. They bore me. With a few exceptions, they are only interested in buying expensive handbags and going to the latest cool bar. I like to date women from outside that privileged bubble. But to do that I have to take certain precautions to make sure I don't get fleeced."

"So, you thought I might try and fleece you if I knew you were wealthy?"

"Not once I'd got to know you. Like I say, I would have told you everything before the next date, but then Charlie, the boy we bumped into, had to show up and ruin everything."

"Who is he, by the way?" asked Zoe.

"He works on reception at our London hotel. Nice lad. I always have a chat to him when I visit. I'll go and see him next week and apologise."

"Will you explain you were incognito with a commoner?"

"Zoe, please try and understand. Would I be ringing now if I wasn't interested and if I didn't trust you? Let's just go on one more date. And this time I will be Michael Britton. I will dress up and you can dress up and I'll give you the full-on Michael Britton experience."

Zoe sighed. "I liked the Michael Braden experience."

"And that's why I want you to give us one more chance.

Let me give you one amazing night before you end things. And if you decide to see me again after that, our next date can be a cheap pizza restaurant, or fish and chips on Brighton Pier."

It's decision time.

"Okay," she said. "One date."

"Amazing. When are you free?"

Zoe wanted to say tonight, but she knew that would sound too keen.

"How about Friday?" Zoe already knew the week was going to drag.

"Perfect," said Michael. "And you're happy for me to arrange everything this time?"

"Why not?"

Is this him taking control? Am I falling for another even richer Doug?

"You won't regret it, Zoe. I'll be in touch before Friday."

As Zoe ended the call, she felt a moment of panic. Was she falling into another mantrap? Giving up her freedom already for the first handsome guy to come along?

It's one date, she told herself, then headed to the kitchen to make a second mug of coffee.

Zoe was right, the next few days did drag. She felt a mixture of excitement at the prospect of another date with Michael, a date where she would finally get to know more about him, and annoyance at having fallen for someone so quickly after Doug. But she couldn't help her emotions. She hadn't planned to bump into a stunningly handsome stranger at the Tate Modern, and she hadn't asked him to track her down and ask her on a second date. She'd even tried to end things, but he'd made a good argument for giving their budding relationship another try. And she certainly couldn't help that the handsome stranger had turned out to be a fabulously wealthy hotelier. He'd gone out of his way to disguise that fact, right down to his scruffy jeans.

Finally, on Thursday she received a message from Michael.

Car will pick you up at 7pm. You said I could take charge of this date, so I have organised everything. Don't worry, no stuffy restaurants.

She had said he could organise this date, so she couldn't get funny that he was doing just that. On this occasion she needed to relax and enjoy the ride.

She was ready and waiting for the car fifteen minutes early, wearing a little black number—sometimes simple was better—and a pair of killer stilettos. She assumed there would be little or no walking involved. She had styled her hair into a loose chignon, which she felt added a bit of relaxed class to her look and—although it had actually taken her about an hour to get right—appeared to have been done as a last-minute consideration.

At seven o'clock precisely, a pristine black car pulled up outside the house. Zoe knew nothing about cars, but she could tell it was expensive. The driver stepped out and walked toward the front door. He was dressed in a full-on chauffeur's uniform, complete with cap. This really was an upgrade from Doug and his taxis.

By the time the driver rang the doorbell, Zoe was already halfway down the stairs. When she opened the door, the chauffeur was waiting at the car.

"Miss Harrison?" he asked.

Michael had obviously remembered her surname from her Facebook page, as she couldn't remember having told him what it was. She smiled at the driver and nodded, ducking down and sliding onto the plush back seat of the car. It smelled of real leather and designer cologne. She wondered if Michael had been sitting where she was a short time ago.

The chauffeur climbed into the driver's seat and turned the ignition key. The engine hummed into life. Zoe sat back and tried to live in the moment rather than attempting to predict what was coming next and analyse all the pros and cons.

She stared out of the window, watching as London passed by. They were heading west, and soon the car was navigating numerous backroads and squares, the houses getting progressively grander. Zoe began to feel panicky. She was out of her depth. Sure, Doug had been well off, but he was from a similar background to her, brought up in the London suburbs by middle class parents. Michael was from a family of millionaires, maybe billionaires, and from what she'd read on the internet in the past few days, their wealth and status dated back several generations.

That doesn't make him better than me.

But it made him different, and different could be scary.

Live in the moment, she reminded herself, as she took a long, deep breath.

"Nearly there, Miss," said the driver.

A few minutes later, they pulled up in a courtyard behind what appeared to be an old-school hotel. It had the grandeur of the Grosvenor House Hotel, but there were no door staff in fancy livery waiting to greet her.

"This is the private entrance, Miss," said the driver, maybe seeing her questioning expression. "The main entrance is around the front, but Mr. Britton asked me to bring you here and tell you to use the elevator just inside the door there and take it right to the top."

As he spoke, the chauffeur climbed out of the car and opened the passenger door for Zoe to make her exit. She did so with as much dignity as possible and thanked him.

"Can I help you to the door?" the driver asked.

"No, I'll be fine," said Zoe.

The cobbled courtyard did make progress in her stilettos challenging, but she managed to reach the door to the hotel without incident, pushing it open and stepping into a small lobby. To her left was an elevator, as the driver had indicated. The door already stood open, so she stepped inside and studied the panel of buttons. The highest floor was the eighth, so she pushed that button and waited for the door to close and the adventure to continue.

As the elevator climbed, she checked herself in the mirror fixed to the back wall. Her hair was still in place and her dress was crease-free. She smiled to make sure there was no lipstick on her teeth. Behind her the elevator door slid open, and Michael stood waiting in the passageway beyond.

"You can't improve on perfection," he said with a grin, as she hastily twirled round to face him rather than her own reflection.

He looked stunning, dressed in a perfectly fitting powder blue suit, brown loafers, and a white shirt, the top two buttons of which were open. His black hair had been swept back from his high forehead, and his dark-blue eyes seemed bigger and more enticing than ever. The confidence that had always been there now seemed even more pronounced, as if before he had been holding it in but now the full force of Michael Britton had been unleashed.

"This is all very mysterious," said Zoe, taking the hand that he offered her and joining him in the passageway.

"This way." Michael led them toward a door at the end of the corridor. He pushed the crossbar handle to open it and gently pulled Zoe through. A gust of cold evening air hit her, and she realised they were standing outside on the roof of the hotel.

"You said you didn't like stuffy places," said Michael. "So I thought we'd have some dinner out here. Everything is set up for us. We won't be bothered by any staff, unless you specifically want something that isn't already here."

"I take it this is one of your hotels," said Zoe, as he led her across the flat roof, weaving round robust chimney breasts and air conditioning units.

"Yes, this is the Britton Grande, set around a five-minute-walk from Park Lane, which is just over there." He pointed to their right, and Zoe took in the view of double-decker buses and black taxis chugging alongside Green Park, which from up here looked much smaller than she'd imagined it to be. Rising beyond that was Buckingham Palace, the Union Jack flag fluttering in the breeze.

"And here we are," said Michael as they turned a corner round a particularly large stack of chimneys.

Zoe released a small gasp of pleasure.

Set up just ahead, with a view across a landscape of chimneys, penthouse apartments and roof gardens, was a little oasis, consisting of a table heaped with trays of food, with fairy lights strung all around. There were heaters to keep out the cold and a beautiful flower display in the centre of the white linen tablecloth. Classical music played softly from a hidden speaker and leading to the table was a carpet of red petals.

"Unstuffy enough for you?" asked Michael.

"It's gorgeous," said Zoe, although the carpet of petals did strike her as more suited to a Valentine treat from a long-term lover than a second date.

I'm living in the moment, remember. This could be our last date. so just enjoy it.

"I decided to go with traditional romantic," said Michael, walking with her to the table. "I figured that if you decided to dump me after tonight, at least I would have had the full hearts and flowers experience with you."

Two chairs had been set up at one end of the table, from which a delicious array of smells was rising. Michael pulled back one of the chairs for Zoe to sit on, then gestured to the row of silver trays, all with domed lids, that stretched the length of the six-foot table.

"I know there isn't much you don't eat, so I've had the kitchen prepare a selection of some of our most popular dishes. Can I help you to a starter? We have escargot in garlic butter, mussels in a cream and onion sauce, grilled asparagus with Parma ham and fresh oysters."

"Yes please," said Zoe.

Michael frowned. "Which would you like?"

"Oh, sorry . . ."

"Or would you like a selection from each?" he added, saving her from embarrassment.

"It does all sound wonderful and it would be a waste not to have a least a little of each."

"I totally agree. I'll do the same."

Zoe watched him lift several lids from various trays and begin to transfer a little from each onto two large plates. Although he was waiting on her, there was nothing servile about him. He operated with a self-assured air.

When they were both sitting and enjoying their starters, Michael began to chat about his family. He was obviously making a point of being open as he'd promised. He told her that the Britton hotel empire had begun with his great grandfather, who had owned a modest little hotel on the south coast, and not even a fashionable part of the south coast. From one hotel, he had grown a small chain, offering five-star service at a more affordable rate than other businesses of a similar standard. When Michael's grandfather had joined the company in the early 1950s, it consisted of around 20 hotels, including the Britton Grande. His grandfather had travelled extensively, discovering new sites for Britton hotels across the world, and soon many of the earlier properties were being sold off in favour of much grander places. This had been the beginning of the Britton empire as it was today.

"What's your favourite country to visit?" Michael asked her.

Zoe pondered her answer as she sipped a chilled glass of Champagne.

"I love Italy. Venice was beautiful and Florence. One of my favourite holidays, though, was in Spain. A group of us stayed in a little villa in the Andalusian Mountains. The views were stunning. We stayed in Barcelona for a few days, too, that was incredible. All that wonderful Gaudi architecture blew me away. Oh and for a bit of glamour, I enjoyed LA. I was on a press trip back when I worked for a woman's magazine. We stayed at Chateau Marmont, which is definitely my favourite hotel ever. So old Hollywood. I'm a sucker for anything related to the silver screen."

Michael smiled. "We have a hotel in LA. Might not quite live up to Chateau Marmont, but in its day it played host to many a star—Elizabeth Taylor, Humphrey Bogart, Vivien Leigh."

"Really?"

"All before my time, of course. I think it still attracts some celebrity clientele, but there's a lot of competition in the city of angels these days."

"Do you travel a lot with your job?" asked Zoe, watching as Michael tipped back his head and sucked an oyster from its shell. It left his lips moist and glistening. His licked them in a way that made her shiver with delight. She hoped he would think she had just reacted to a cold breeze blowing across the roof.

"I try and get around to all our hotels during the year," he replied. "But we have an excellent team of people who keep everything running smoothly. My belief is that a great business leader makes himself, or herself, dispensable."

"Sounds very wise."

Michael suddenly fixed her with his gaze. Those dark eyes really were intoxicating.

"Thank you for coming tonight," he said. "I thought I may have blown it."

"Thank you for making it so lovely."

"We haven't even had the main course yet. Would you like me to run through the options, or shall I just assume you'll want a bit of everything?"

She laughed. "You know me so well already."

They chatted into the early hours, with Michael continuing to ask her questions about herself, but also sharing anecdotes about his family. His father, he said, was a great lover of horses and spent much of his time at the race track these days, happy for his sons to look after the running of the family business. Zoe cautiously asked what Samuel's role was within Britton Hotels and whether it was proving difficult to work with him since the situation with Lucy had arisen.

"Samuel is the marketing director," explained Michael. "He enjoys that side of things. Officially he reports to me, but he earns as much as I do and rarely consults with me before making a major decision. It was hard working with him before the Lucy thing. Now it's even more unpleasant. But luckily he is good at his job, so at least I know he won't do anything to drive the business into the ground."

Zoe glanced at her watch. "God, it's two in the morning. I feel like I only just got here."

"I hope that's a good sign."

"It certainly is, but I really should get home."

In truth, she'd have been happy talking for another few hours, but the wine had gone to her head and she didn't want to do anything she would regret the next day.

"There's a bed for you here if you would prefer to stay," said Michael.

"No!" blurted Zoe, standing. Her chair made a rude scraping sound on the roof surface.

Michael raised his eyebrows. "I meant you could take one of the empty rooms."

"Oh, right."

How to make a complete fool of myself.

"Not that the thought of trying to seduce you hasn't crossed my mind," continued Michael, also standing so that she had a view of his entire, perfect form. "But that's not what tonight was about. I wanted to show you that I could be Michael the rich hotelier and not be a dickhead."

"Well, you've succeeded."

"I'm glad. In that case, I will seduce you on our next date. If there is one. I'd like there to be."

"Me too," she said, as he wrapped an arm around her waist and led her back to the fire exit door. She wanted to get even closer to him, to have him wrap both arms around her and pull her into the heat of his body, kiss her with those sensual lips while she breathed in the scent of him.

In the lift he turned to her and smiled. "How about a goodnight kiss, at least?"

Zoe nodded and closed her eyes. She felt his lips brush hers and deliver a gentle kiss that left just a trace of moisture. It was over in a second, but Zoe felt dizzy with passion.

She opened her eyes to see his face still close to hers, his gaze flicking across her features as if waiting for some indication that she wanted more. She could feel that he was aroused, his hardness pressed against her and she wanted to forget about being cautious. It would have been so easy to just unzip his fly and free his member, grip its thickness in her hand and pleasure him. She longed to see the look in those eyes as she brought him to orgasm.

The elevator door pinged open and after the briefest hesitation, Zoe stepped out into the small lobby. She could see the black car parked outside in the courtyard.

Michael remained in the elevator. He stood with his hands in his pockets, one side of his mouth upturned into a half-smile. Zoe's glance strayed briefly to the enticing bulge in his trousers, then back to his face.

"Goodnight, Zoe. I'll call you tomorrow."

"Goodnight," she replied as the elevator door closed.

She headed outside, slightly surprised he hadn't escorted

her to the car. She felt hot and dizzy, as if they had shared far more than just a quick kiss. And as she climbed into the back of the car, part of her wished they had.

CHAPTER FOUR

"Earth to Zoe!"

Zoe looked up from her glass of wine, realizing she'd been staring into it for about five minutes and completely ignoring her friend, Rachael.

"Were you thinking about him again?" asked Racheal, a pretty, plump redhead.

"Sorry. I should know better, shouldn't I?" said Zoe. "I just can't believe he hasn't called, after going to all that effort to find me and then convince me to see him again. Either I was just so boring on our last date, or he's moved on to his next challenge."

"It's only been a few days."

"He said he'd call on Saturday."

"Maybe something cropped up at work."

"He could have texted."

"He is a CEO of a massive company," Rachael pointed out. "Who knows what pressure he's under."

"It takes a few seconds to write a text. Let's face it, why would someone like him chase after someone like me? He obviously just saw it as a bit of sport. Trick the girl from suburbia into thinking she's caught the interest of a wealthy hotelier and then just drop her."

"I'm sure it's not like that," said Rachael, glancing around the bar they'd chosen to meet in. "There's a cute guy over there giving you the eye."

"I'm not interested. This time I really am swearing off men for at least six months."

Rachael drained her glass. "Do you want another one?"

"I'd better not. I have a deadline tomorrow. I should get an early night."

"No problem," said Rachael. "In that case, I may go and chat to that cute guy, because I think it's actually me he's giving the eye to."

Zoe laughed. "Go for it!"

She waited to make sure Rachael and the guy, who was indeed very cute and probably a good five years younger than Rachael, were chatting happily, then headed for home.

Why couldn't she just have fun like Rachael? Why did she always have to fall for guys that played games with her? Was she an easy target?

Her phone bleeped as she arrived at her flat. She glanced at the screen. It was a message from Michael. Her stomach clenched and her heart fluttered. She prepared herself for the worst.

Zoe! What a few days I've had. So sorry I didn't call on Saturday. I've had a real nightmare. Problems at our hotel in LA. Kept meaning to call or message then something else would happen and before I knew it another day had gone. Anyway, things are under control now and you are the first person I'm contacting. I had a great night and I'd love to see you again. I'm currently in L.A., staying at your beloved Chateau Marmont. Care to join me?

Zoe read the message several times. Was he serious about her joining him? Did he think she could just drop everything and fly to LA? He really was arrogant.

She kept her reply short.

Glad you are okay. Hope everything works out with the hotel. Give me a call when you get back.

Aloof enough, but without burning any bridges.

He responded almost immediately.

You don't fancy a long weekend at Chateau Marmont then? If you can get next Monday and Tuesday off work, there's a flight on Friday evening I could book you on. Too much too soon?

He really was serious.

The reality was that once she sent through the latest batch of content to the website tomorrow, she had a gap of a few weeks before the next lot was due, so she could easily take a couple of days off. It would be perfect timing. But did she want to be that woman that ran to a man when he clicked his fingers?

It's a free trip to LA and I'd be staying at my favourite hotel in the world. I'm not selling my soul to the Devil. I like this guy. I should have an adventure.

She lay on her bed, phone still clutched in her hand, staring at the ceiling. Chances like this didn't come along twice. maybe this thing with Michael would be a short-lived fling. Perhaps she was just a bit of fun for him while he got over Lucy, but why not just go with it? Live a little. In a few years' time she might be settled down with a husband who worked in a bank and two kids. At least she'd always have the memory of when a millionaire flew her to LA for a long weekend of . . . of what? Would he expect her to sleep with him? Would she mind if he did?

Oh God, I don't know what to say!

Finally she made a decision and typed her response, pressing send before she could change her mind.

Obviously, I'd love to come, but it's too much! You'll have to let me at least pay towards the cost. But, yes, if you're serious, I'd love to join you.

She waited, heart pounding so hard the bed was vibrating.

His reply came through.

Don't be ridiculous. I invited you, so this is on me. You can pay for the trip to Brighton and the fish and chips. I will send you a link to the flight details when I've booked it. Make sure you have your visa waiver thing up to date. See you at the Chateau. x

Oh my God! I'm actually doing it.

Zoe clutched the phone to her chest and grinned.

Zoe had expected to be too excited and nervous to sleep on the flight, but she hadn't counted on just how comfortable flying first class would be. Within minutes of extending her seat into a bed and pulling the soft blanket up to her chin, she was asleep. She didn't wake until the plane was coming in to land. She was glad she'd eaten and enjoyed a glass of complementary Champagne before lying down. After all, she might never fly first class again.

She'd half expected Michael to be waiting for her at arrivals, but instead a middle-aged woman in a chauffeur's uniform stood holding up a placard with her name written on it.

She spent the half-hour drive to the hotel in a dream, and when she saw the fairy-tale towers of Chateau Marmont rising from the side of Sunset Boulevard, she almost had to pinch herself to make sure she was actually awake. She'd never expected to see this place again.

The driver pulled the car into the driveway up to the main entrance, and a member of staff immediately ran to help her with her bag. Zoe was glad she'd remembered to bring some dollar bills with her to use as tips.

She followed the bell boy up the short flight of stairs to the reception. She remembered it all so well from her last visit—the dramatic baroque décor, all with a sheen of Hollywood glitz. A buzz of conversation rose from the outside bar behind her, and she wondered if she and Michael would sit and enjoy a drink out there later, maybe partake in a spot of star spotting.

"Good evening, do you have a reservation with us?" asked the beaming receptionist, who like many hotel and restaurant staff in LA, looked like a top model.

Zoe hesitated. She hadn't actually confirmed with Michael whose name he'd booked her room under—assuming he'd booked her a separate room and wasn't expecting her to sleep with him.

"My friend made the reservation for me," she said. "Michael Britton."

"Oh yes, here it is." The receptionist beamed. "You're staying in one of our suites, Miss Harrison." She handed Zoe a key, and it was an old-fashioned key, not a card. "Jake here will help you with your bags."

Jake, the eager bellboy smiled and led the way to the elevator. Zoe remembered how much she'd loved the elevators on her last visit. They were pure art deco, complete with an old-fashioned dial floor indicator, which was currently ticking down from 4 to 1.

"After you, Mam," said Jake with a nod and Zoe stepped into the elevator.

She wondered if the receptionist knew her situation—that she had flown out to be with a man she barely knew and allowed him to pay for everything.

Of course she doesn't know, how could she?

She felt another wave of panic. Had she made a massive mistake? Would she feel indebted to Michael now that she allowed him to fund all this?

She and Jake were standing outside a sturdy-looking wooden door. She'd been so deep in thought that she couldn't even remember leaving the elevator. Jake was looking at her expectantly.

"Oh, thank you." She handed him several dollar bills, and he disappeared with a nod and a smile.

From the other side of the door, Zoe heard a raised voice. It was Michael, and he sounded enraged.

"This should never have happened, and I pay you a lot of money to make sure things like this don't happen. We have never had a Britton hotel closed down because of a health scare. The publicity and loss of business will be very damaging. I should fire you, but if I do that, I'll be letting you walk away, when you need to step up and take responsibility. Now get back over there and start doing that!"

The door opened and a man of around thirty stood staring at her for a moment. He looked like he was about to cry.

"Excuse me," he said, slipping past her and hurrying toward the elevators.

"Zoe, you're here already."

Michael was standing in the middle of a spacious living area. He was dressed in dark-blue jeans, a white shirt and a light-grey sports jacket. Every item fitted him perfectly, showing every curve of every muscle, but in a subtle, sexy way.

"Hi," she said, still standing in the corridor.

"I'm sorry about that." Michael strode toward her. "He was the senior restaurant manager of our hotel. I needed him to know how upset I am about the situation."

"I think he got the message."

Michael kissed her on the cheek and took her bag.

"Do you want to unpack and freshen up before I take you for a late dinner?" he asked, wheeling the case through to an adjoining room. Zoe followed.

"I can unpack later, if you want to eat," she said, glancing round the bedroom for signs of Michael's belongings. But a quick peak in the en suite bathroom and the wardrobe revealed nothing to suggest he was sleeping in this room.

Michael flashed her a knowing smile. "I booked one of the two-bed suites."

"It's wonderful," said Zoe. "Thanks so much for doing this. I feel like I'm in a dream."

"I've been feeling like I was in a nightmare for the past few days," said Michael. "But now it feels more like a dream."

He took her hand and pulled her toward him, kissing her on the lips. Zoe wanted to open her mouth and welcome his tongue, but she broke the kiss and smiled.

"Give me ten minutes to have a quick wash and brush my teeth and I'll be with you," she said, fighting her first impulse, which was to fall onto the bed, pulling Michael with her.

"No problem." Michael kissed her again, before leaving the room.

Zoe stood for a moment, relishing the tingling sensation his lips had left on hers.

Over dinner in a spacious, modern restaurant set on the top floor of a private club in the commercial district of LA, Michael explained what had been going on that had caused him so much stress.

Trying not to be distracted by the view across a shimmering swimming pool to the sprawling cityscape of LA, Zoe listened and sympathised. Michael told her how on the Saturday after their date he'd received a call saying that there had been a major health and safety issue at the LA Hotel. In the space of one evening, five guests had discovered a cockroach in their meals while eating in the hotel restaurant.

"Nothing like this has ever happened at one of our hotels. We are so fastidious about cleanliness and health and safety in general," said Michael. "Anyway, the hotel had to close down while the officials came in to do a check of the entire premises. They found nothing. Not one roach, not a single mouse dropping. They said the hygiene standards throughout were excellent."

"So how . . ." began Zoe.

"Exactly. I can only assume it was sabotage."

"Who by? A competitor? An angry employee?"

"I look after my employees," said Michael. "I expect them to perform, but as long as they show me commitment and loyalty, I make sure they are properly rewarded at every level. A contented team is what carries a business."

"I agree totally. I was just wondering who could have got close enough to the kitchen to plant cockroaches in the food and why they'd want to. Have you reported it to the police?"

Michael shook his head. "Our PR department put out a

release including sections of the hygiene report, which speaks for itself. If the police get involved, this could drag on for months, and we need it to be forgotten as soon as possible. Anyway, I didn't fly you all this way to talk about roaches. It's been dealt with, and I want to just relax for a few days before heading back to London."

"I'll drink to that," said Zoe, raising her Champagne glass. He did the same and clinked his glass against hers.

"It's really good to see you," he said.

"And you. I was wondering if our date on the roof really was going to be our first and last."

He reached across the table and squeezed her hand. "Why would you think that?"

"I'm not exactly from the same world as you. I dip in and out of glamorous places like this, if I'm lucky enough to get invited on a press trip or whisked away by handsome men who own hotel groups."

Michael laughed. "I don't want someone from my world. I told you that."

"What about Lucy, what was her background?" asked Zoe.

Michael shrugged. "Her father is a surgeon, her mother runs a theatrical agency."

"Well, my dad worked for a building society, managing one small branch near where we lived for thirty years, and my mum flitted from one retail job to another. And I mean she worked in shops, serving people—she wasn't part of central office management or anything. Like I say, we are from completely different worlds. It sounds like Lucy came from a very different social background than me."

"You're the one that seems hung up on social backgrounds," said Michael, gazing at her with a penetrating stare. "I don't care what your parents did for a living. They must be decent people, because they helped make you the person you are, and I really like that person."

Zoe blushed. "I'm not that insecure. But you can see why I may be slightly nervous about where this is going."

"Can we just agree to enjoy where we are now?" said Michael, still staring at her intently. "If at any time either of us feels the need for some reassurance as to what the future holds, then we can speak up and be honest about it. All I can say is that I have no interest in dating anyone else right now. God, even if I did want to see several women at once, I wouldn't have time."

"Okay," said Zoe. "It's a deal."

"How about we have coffee and brandy back at the Chateau?" suggested Michael. "We can sit on our balcony and take in the view of the Hollywood Hills."

"Sounds perfect," said Zoe.

And it really did.

Zoe sipped her brandy, enjoying the warmth as it slid down her throat and stared out over the Hollywood Hills. They were swathed in shadow, with the occasional light shining from a distant window. She imagined famous actors and actresses staying up late to learn their lines for a shoot the following day. Perhaps one of them would glance up from their script and see the light from their hotel suite, maybe even catch a glimpse of her and Michael sitting side by side on the balcony and wonder what their story was. They'd probably assume they were a couple, taking a vacation together, which in a way they were, although it all still felt like a dream. Only a couple of weeks ago Michael had been a friendly stranger inviting her for lunch in a riverside pub, and now they were sitting on a balcony at the Chateau Marmont, drinking brandy and enjoying the comfortable silence.

She wondered if there might be some awkwardness when they came to say goodnight, which would be soon, as she was so tired, despite having slept on the plane.

Would Michael, as he'd suggested on their last date, try and seduce her? If he did, would she resist him? She was a grown woman, and it was obvious she was attracted to him.

I didn't travel thousands of miles to be with someone I just like as a friend.

What could be more romantic than making love to a gorgeous man in a hotel room steeped in the history of Hollywood?

But something made her want to wait. Despite all this, Michael still needed to prove to her that she was more than just a bit of fun between serious girlfriends. If she slept with him tonight, she knew she would fall for him in a big way, and if he didn't feel the same, she was going to get hurt. Better to be careful, play the part of the chaste heroine for a bit longer and see how things developed between them.

She yawned and stood up. "I'm heading to bed."

Michael stared up at her, and looking down into those blue eyes she was tempted to forget everything she had just been thinking and allow herself to be seduced. Let those full lips kiss her mouth and neck, that tongue trace a line from her neck to her breasts, gently teasing each nipple until she couldn't bear any more.

He stood and pulled her to him. "Thank you for a lovely evening," he said, then kissed her, and this time she opened her mouth a fraction and his tongue probed between her lips. Their kissing grew in passion, Michael's hand dropping to the small of her back, pulling her closer. She felt how hard he was and groaned with desire. She wanted him inside her.

Take me to the bedroom!

Michael pulled away, planting a final kiss on her forehead. "You should get some sleep. I thought tomorrow we could drive out to Santa Monica. There's a great seafood restaurant I think you'll like. They do really big portions."

Zoe tried to control her breathing and the pounding of her heart. Was he really not going to take this further? At least give her the chance to say no, to feel virtuous? Now she just felt rejected.

"That sounds great," she said and turned to head inside.

"You know I want you," he said to her back.

That's more like it.

"There's no rush," she replied, and with all the will power she possessed, she headed for her bedroom, closing the door behind her.

Chapter Five

The crab cakes were delicious, melting in her mouth before she even needed to chew. Their flavour seemed intensified by the salty fragrance of the sea air and the sound of waves lapping at the beach below.

The restaurant was buzzy and full of families and real people rather than the model-like inhabitants of LA. Zoe was enjoying the relaxed atmosphere. Much as she loved the glamour of LA, she felt more at home here in Santa Monica, eating too much seafood and watching the seagulls swoop down to steal from those brave enough to try and eat food on the beach.

She realised Michael was watching her and smiling.

"What?" she asked between mouthfuls of crab.

"Nothing, it's just nice to be on a date with a woman who enjoys her food."

"I love food. I love posh food, junk food and everything in between."

"And yet you're not the size of a house."

"I jog a lot," said Zoe between mouthfuls. "I run nearly every day, even if I don't feel like it, because the thought of having to watch what I eat is far worse than running in the rain, or with a hangover."

"It makes a nice change, that's all."

"I suppose Lucy eats like a bird."

Michael frowned. "Let's not talk about her."

"Sorry. I won't mention her again."

"Did you want anything else, or do you fancy a walk along

the beach?" asked Michael.

"No, I'm full." Zoe wondered if it would be rude to lick her plate and deciding yes it would be.

Michael excused himself and disappeared among the crowds in the restaurant. He was wearing a pair of dark-blue shorts, and Zoe admired his legs as he walked away. The thighs and calves were toned and tanned, and the shorts hugged his butt perfectly. Zoe fanned herself with a menu. It really was a hot day.

Michael reappeared moments later.

"Let's go then," he said.

"Did you pay?" asked Zoe. "I was going to treat you."

"Treat me another time," said Michael, gazing across the beach, using his hand as a shield against the blazing sun. He'd left his sunglasses at the hotel.

Zoe stood, unhooking her handbag from the back of the chair. "You say that every time. I don't want to be a kept woman."

"This whole trip is my treat," said Michael. "Just relax and enjoy it."

Part of Zoe wanted to do just that—be the pampered princess for a few days—but it didn't sit comfortably with her. Doug had earned more than she did, but she had still regularly treated him or at least shared the cost of their meals out.

This guy is worth millions. Just enjoy it.

As they walked down the sandy walkway to the beach, Michael took her hand. Warmth flooded through her, and she felt a surge of desire for him. She wasn't sure how much longer she could resist going to bed with him, or if she should even be resisting.

The sun was beautifully warm and the air dry. There was none of the heavy humidity that came with hot days in London. The sea was a shade of turquoise, joining the clear blue sky at the horizon. Zoe took a deep breath and squeezed Michael's hand. This really was idyllic, if she could just stop over-thinking it.

They strolled along the beach, winding their way through clusters of sunbathers and families struggling to protect their picnics from the scavenging gulls.

"Are you glad you came?" asked Michael.

"Yes of course I am, it's been wonderful. Going back to real life will be hard, now I've seen how the other half live."

"I'd like to see where you live. Maybe you could cook my dinner one night."

"I don't cook as well as I eat. But I will give it a go."

"It's a date then."

"But my flat is nothing special."

"I'm sure it is."

Why was she putting her flat down like that? She'd always loved it, and it was special. She'd bought it five years earlier with her own money as a deposit, saved up over more than a decade and she was proud that she'd managed to buy a property in London with no help from her parents or a rich boyfriend. So it might not be as impressive as wherever Michael lived, but it was her home, and she shouldn't be ashamed of it.

"Actually, it is," she said finally. "And I'd love you to come over. We'll fix up a date when we get back."

Michael glanced at his watch. "Unfortunately I have an online meeting in a couple of hours, so are you okay to head back to the hotel soon? I can get the driver to pick us up about a ten-minute walk from here."

"Yes, that's fine." Zoe tried not to show her disappointment. She hadn't realised there was such a short time-limit on their day together.

"It will only be for about an hour, and then we can go for a cocktail in the hotel bar or sit by the pool and sip Champagne until it gets dark."

"That's sounds lovely and I could actually do with a nap.

The jetlag is kicking in."

She did try and sleep when they got back, but she could hear Michael and his colleagues talking in the main living room, plus her head was racing with all kinds of conflicting thoughts. One voice was saying she should enjoy the adventure, the other that she was letting herself be ruled by her feelings. The sensible inner voice said that she was going to get hurt, the other that she should make the most of Michael and his generosity.

Be independent! screamed one voice. *Go with the flow!* shouted the other.

By the time Michael tapped on the bedroom door, she felt more tired than when she'd gone to lie down an hour and a half earlier.

"All done," he said softly. "Fancy sitting by the pool for a while?"

"Sure," she replied sleepily. "Give me ten minutes."

"No rush, darling," said Michael, pulling the door closed.

Darling!

Was that how he really thought of her, or had it been a slip of the tongue? Maybe that was his preferred term of endearment for Lucy and he'd used it instinctively.

Let it go. Don't read too much into it.

She pulled a very lightweight summer dress from the wardrobe and held it up against her body, appraising herself in mirror on the inside of the wardrobe door. There was no way she was wearing a bathing costume, but this was nice alternative. It was made of a sheer white fabric, sleeveless, and came down to just above her knees. She'd pair it with some simple sandals.

When she emerged from her room a few minutes later, she found Michael standing in the middle of the living room, wearing a pair of tight red shorts and some deck shoes. He looked stunning. His muscular chest was smooth and tanned, the nipples hard and dark. His stomach was flat with the hint of a six-pack rippling under the taut skin.

"Ready?" he asked, and it was all she could do not to pull him into the bedroom and beg him to make love to her.

"Let's go," she replied, her voice more high-pitched than normal.

They made their way down to the ground floor, stepping out of the elevator just a short walk from the gate that led to the pool area. There were a number of people lying next to the pool on sun loungers, although no one looked familiar—no major A-listers.

Lush greenery surrounded the area around the pool, blocking out the sight and sounds of Sunset Boulevard and creating the impression that they were wandering through an oasis, complete with poolside bar and telephones from which you could order anything to be delivered to you while you enjoyed the sun.

They found two loungers at the far side of the pool, and Zoe was happy to stretch out and feel the heat of the sun beating down on her.

"I hope you have sun cream on," said Michael, who was spritzing his legs with lotion as he spoke, massaging it into the skin. Zoe imagined her hands rubbing lotion into those muscular calves and her stomach fluttered.

"I put some factor thirty on in my room," she replied.

"Planning on keeping your English rose complexion then?" said Michael, now basting his chest and shoulders.

"Yes." Zoe was worried her voice would quaver if she said any more.

"So," said Michael as he lay down. "What would be your dream job? Assuming money was no object."

"Are you interviewing me? Zoe pushed her sunglasses down from the top of her head over her eyes, then also lay flat on her back.

"Just curious."

"I guess I'd be a full-time writer."

"What would you write?"

"I've always wanted to write a real blockbuster, some kind of family saga full of lust and intrigue."

"Why haven't you?" asked Michael.

"Because I've been too busy being a journalist or a PR or a content writer," Zoe replied.

"And you didn't have any free time to write your steamy novel?"

Zoe paused. "I suppose I could have made the time."

"Too busy eating?"

"Shut up." Zoe laughed.

"You should start writing it when you get home," said Michael. "Maybe it could begin where a hot young woman meets an equally hot guy in an art gallery . . ."

"Who pretends to be a poor little hotel worker.'

"No, that guy sounds like a dick."

Zoe laughed and turned on her side to face Michael, who, perhaps hearing her shift in position, was also looking at her through a pair of designer sunglasses, which had probably cost more than her entire wardrobe of clothes back in the hotel suite.

"What about you?" she asked. "If you had a choice would you still be a hotelier, or is there another career Michael Britton would have liked to follow?"

"Well, I love art, which is why you met me at the Tate Modern, but I can't actually paint or make things."

"Nor could a lot of the artists responsible for the exhibits at the Tate Modern," said Zoe.

"True. So maybe I could just bluff my way through it."

"You could do a Tracey Emin and just move something from your childhood town and stick it in an art gallery."

"Or I could put a cow in a tank of formaldehyde. No, even

better, I could stick my brother in a tank of formaldehyde. There would at least be a good story behind that piece."

"That's a bit macabre."

"Yes, sorry. Forget I said that. Anyway, I don't think being an artist is a realistic option, so I'll go for racing driver instead."

"Do you even know how to drive?" asked Zoe.

"Yes! Why would you ask that?" exclaimed Michael, propping himself on one elbow and scrutinising her.

Zoe laughed. "Because you have drivers take you everywhere."

"I do not have drivers take me everywhere. Only when I may want to enjoy a drink. I quite often drive myself."

"Okay, I'm sorry," said Zoe. "So, you'd be a racing driver. That sounds exciting, but dangerous."

"That just about sums me up," said Michael, raising his eyebrows and lying down again.

Zoe giggled. She was enjoying this more playful side to him.

A waiter appeared at the end of their loungers carrying a tray containing a bottle of Champagne in an ice bucket and two glasses.

"Oh good," said Michael. "I ordered it from the suite before we came down."

"Lovely," said Zoe.

"You can just leave it here and we'll pour for ourselves," Michael said to the waiter, nodding to a small table between their sun loungers."

As the waiter left, Michael sat up, swinging his legs around so that his bare feet rested on the floor. He lifted the Champagne bottle from the bucket and poured them each a glass. Zoe sat up to accept hers.

"Cheers!" Michael touched his glass to hers. "And thanks for a lovely day."

"No, thank you," said Zoe. "I'm having a brilliant time."

"Two more nights to go yet."

Will I sleep with him on one of them? Will I actually get to see that perfect body completely naked?

"And several more eating occasions," added Michael.

He thinks I'm obsessed with food.

"On that subject, what do you fancy for dinner tonight?" he asked.

"Oh, I can't even think about food after that lunch."

"Try."

"A huge burger with fries and pickles," said Zoe.

"That's my girl." He laughed. "I know just the place and it's very chilled. You'll like it. Full of real American people enjoying their meat and fries!"

"Perfect," said Zoe. "But I couldn't eat for a couple of hours at least."

"Not even a few nibbles to go with the Champagne?"

"No!"

Michael leaned forward, placed a hand on her thigh and kissed her on the mouth. "I'm only teasing."

As soon as he sat back, Zoe missed the pressure and heat of his hand. She wanted his hands to touch her all over while he kissed her passionately with his gorgeous full lips. She took a gulp of Champagne and pulled her legs back onto the lounger, curling them round her bottom. She surveyed the other people around the pool. A woman emerged from the mini jungle to their right, where the exclusive bungalows were set. She was tall with the longest legs Zoe had ever seen and a mass of shining blonde hair.

"Oh my God," Zoe whispered.

"What?" Michael followed the direction of her gaze.

"It's her! The actress from that TV show."

"Okay."

"You know, Bella something. The show's about a law firm and she plays the really bitchy one."

"Oh her!" said Michael. "Oh yes, I like her, she's hot."

"I wonder how much is really her, though, and how much is down to a good surgeon."

Michael smirked. "She has nothing on you, if that's any consolation."

"Oh come off it. Look how everyone around the pool, male and female, is staring at her. She's gorgeous."

"So are you. You just have no idea how gorgeous you are, while she does, and that makes other people notice her."

"Okay, Doctor Britton, thanks for the consultation, I think our time is up."

"Fair enough," said Michael. "I promise I will never tell you how gorgeous I think you are again."

"You better not," said Zoe with a half-smile.

"So complex," sighed Michael, sipping his Champagne.

Zoe looked from the huge burger to Michael, then down at the burger again.

"Are you trying to work out how to eat it and still look attractive?" asked Michael.

This would definitely be a test of just how much Michael liked her she thought as she picked up the mammoth double-decker burger with both hands and took a large bite out of it. She felt ketchup and grease dribble down her chin, but she didn't care. It was truly the most delicious thing she had ever tasted.

"That is incredible," she said, placing the culinary delight back on the plate and wiping her mouth with a paper napkin from a metal dispenser.

Michael laughed. "I feel as if our relationship just moved to another level."

"How will you eat yours?" asked Zoe, eyeing Michael's equally full plate.

"Like a real man." Michael grabbed his burger in one hand

and took a huge bite, making growling noises to show his appreciation as he chewed.

Fortunately the music in the restaurant was loud—the juke box was currently blaring out *Living on a Prayer*—so Michael's performance went unnoticed by the other patrons. Also they were tucked in a faux leather booth, which offered a certain amount of privacy.

Zoe grinned and went in for a second bite, closing her eyes to relish the combination of flavours.

Good job I'm not trying to convince him I'm a sophisticated woman of mystery.

When she opened her eyes, Zoe discovered there was a stunningly attractive blonde woman standing next to their booth. Her long hair was fixed in a loose bun and she was dressed in a perfectly fitting Chanel suit.

"Lucy!" exclaimed Michael, as Zoe grabbed another napkin and frantically wiped her mouth.

"Hello, Michael," Lucy said in a clipped English accent.

"What are you doing here?" Michael demanded.

"I'm here with Samuel. He wanted to eat somewhere unpretentious and down-market. It wasn't my choice. He said not to disturb you, but I felt rude just walking past your table without saying hi."

"But what are you both doing in LA?" asked Michael.

"Same as you," said Lucy. "Your father asked Samuel to fly out and make sure everything was being handled properly."

"I'm here," said Michael, his voice like ice.

"Yes," said Lucy, glancing at Zoe.

"Hi." Zoe held out her hand. "Good to meet you, I'm Zoe."

Lucy nodded and made a feeble attempt at shaking hands.

"Well, I won't disturb you any longer," she said. "Samuel will be waiting for me."

"Get him to call me first thing," said Michael, his voice not thawing any.

Lucy nodded and strode off toward the exit. The juke box

was playing *Hound Dog* by Elvis, which pleased Zoe no end.

"How dare he," fumed Michael, pushing his plate away.

"Your brother, you mean?" asked Zoe, wondering if she, too, needed to finish eating.

"He's trying to undermine me. He obviously convinced Father that he should fly out. There is absolutely no need for the marketing director to be here."

"I thought you were in charge of the company."

"I'm the CEO on paper, but Father still calls the shots and Samuel knows it. What's his game?"

He fell silent, staring into space, obviously brooding.

"So, that's Lucy," said Zoe.

"What?" Michael returned his gaze to her. "Oh yes, that's Lucy. She wasn't always that much of a bitch. Being with Samuel obviously disagrees with her."

"I wouldn't say bitchy exactly. Just cold."

"That bastard," murmured Michael, draining his bottle of beer.

"We should go. You need to call your brother and have it out with him."

"What about your burger?"

"I've had enough," lied Zoe.

"I'm so sorry." Michael waved their waitress over. "I was having such a great time, too."

Zoe gave her delicious burger a final, longing look as they stood to leave. They had walked to the restaurant as it was so close to the hotel, and they walked back, too, neither speaking. Zoe could feel the anger rising from Michael.

When they got back to their suite, Zoe went to her room to give Michael some privacy, but she could hear his raised voice anyway. After about twenty minutes the shouting stopped and Michael knocked on her door. Zoe opened it and offered him a sympathetic smile.

"I'm sorry," he said.

"It's fine," Zoe assured him.

"No, I mean I'm sorry, but I have to head back early."

"Why?" Zoe felt as if her heart had dropped to her feet.

"After I finished talking with Samuel, I got a call from my operations director, Dave Mills. I knew something was wrong because it's the middle of the night in England. There's been an outbreak of salmonella at the Grande. It's been closed down pending an inspection by the HSA."

"You have got to be joking. This can't be a coincidence."

"I don't know what's going on. I just feel so bad that I have to leave. Do you want to stay here on your own, or would you prefer to fly back with me tomorrow morning?"

Zoe imagined LA would be a lonely place without Michael.

"I definitely want to come back with you," she said. "If that's okay."

"Of course it is. I'll contact the airline now. The flight leaves at seven in the morning, so we'll need to be in the car by four. Again, I'm so sorry."

"Don't worry. Go and get some sleep and I'll see you in the morning."

As soon as her bedroom door was closed, tears rolled down Zoe's face. It had all been going so well. Maybe this was a sign that she was out of her depth, that she needed to just be grateful for what she had and stop trying to pretend she was the kind of woman who could make Michael Britton happy.

She glanced at the digital clock next to the bed. It was only nine o'clock, but she might as well try and sleep if they were leaving in the early hours of the morning. She wiped the tears from her cheeks and began to pack her case.

Chapter Six

For the first two days after arriving back in London, Michael called her regularly. But by day three the calls had been replaced by text messages and for the past week Zoe hadn't heard from him at all.

"It does sound like he's got a lot to deal with," pointed out her friend Jen, who Zoe had been chatting to over the phone for the past half an hour.

"I know that," said Zoe. "I'm not even annoyed with him, because I understand he's probably just too busy to call. But I just don't think I want to deal with it. I went straight from Doug to seeing Michael and it was so intense and magical for a brief time and now I'm feeling anxious and wondering if he'll ever call again. I don't want to feel like that. I swore off men because I didn't want to feel like this anymore. I know it makes me sound needy, but I'm just not the kind of woman that can wait around for days for a call. I need to know everything is okay or my mind starts working overtime. I just don't think I can date someone like Michael."

"So, are you going to end it?" asked Jen.

"I think I am. I can't believe I'm saying that, but I think I am. If I know it's over I can just move on and stop checking my phone for missed calls every hour."

"You could always ring him."

"I have done. I left a message the other day and I just got a one-line text back saying he'd call me when things were less mad. That was a week ago."

"It's up to you. But if I had a gorgeous looking multi-millionaire interested in me, I'm not sure I'd be so quick to end things. If I wasn't married to John, obviously."

"I know it sounds mad, but I also know what I'm like. I'll get more and more anxious the longer he leaves it before calling, and then when he does eventually call, I'll end up getting angry with him, when he won't really have done anything wrong. I don't want to get into that cycle with a man again."

"Well, I'm sure you'll make the right decision," said Jen. "I have to go now, I need to pick the kids up from school, but let me know how it goes."

After finishing the call, Zoe did some work, finally shutting down her laptop at 6pm and running herself a bath. She picked up her mobile phone while she waited for the bath to fill. Should she just end it with a text?

I can't just finish with him by text message. He flew me first class to LA, for God's sake.

Zoe sighed and instead called Michael's number. As expected, she went through to voicemail. It was decision time.

"Hi Michael," she said after the beep. "Listen, I wanted to talk to you rather than leave a message but you're never available. I'm so sorry to do this, but I think it's best if we don't see each other again. I will always remember LA, and I am so grateful to you for making my dream to stay at Chateau Marmont again come true, but I just don't think we are right for each other. Whatever you say, we come from different worlds, and I think I just want to go back to my world and be on my own for a while. That was the plan before I met you. So good luck with everything that's going on at the moment. I hope it all gets sorted out, and take care of yourself. Bye, Michael."

When she ended the call, her hand was shaking. She could hardly believe she'd done it, but she'd needed to take the lead, end things on her terms. She'd hoped it would make her feel empowered, but she just felt wretched.

She undressed and climbed into the bath, sinking beneath

the bubbles and closing her eyes. The warmth of the water helped ease her stress a little, but she couldn't relax. Had he listened to the message? How would he feel when he heard it? How could she have ended things like that after everything he'd done for her?

Why did I end it at all? I could have just waited and seen how things developed. Oh God, what have I done!

Zoe slapped the surface of the bathwater with both hands in frustration. She'd let her anxiety get the better of her again—ended a blossoming relationship before it had been given a chance to develop, all because Michael hadn't called her for a few days. His business was in crisis—what did she expect?

She climbed out of the bath and pulled on a robe, then shuffled through to the living-room, where she flung herself, still wet, onto the sofa. She felt utterly miserable. Michael would think she was a needy brat, ending things just because he hadn't been able to make her the centre of attention while he struggled to safe his family business.

She'd almost forgotten how insecure she got at the beginning of a relationship, when things were still uncertain. With Michael, the feelings were intensified to a new extreme, because she had fallen for him so quickly and so heavily.

Maybe it was for the best. Perhaps she really did need some time alone to think about what she actually wanted from a relationship and from life in general. If being with Michael was making her feel like this after just a few dates, maybe it was a sign of how their relationship would develop. That was the problem with anxiety—she was always thinking ahead and about what could go wrong, rather than enjoying the moment.

Well, she'd made the decision now and there was no going back after leaving that message.

Michael called an hour later. Zoe, still lying on the sofa, stared at his name for a moment before deciding to accept the call. She was prepared for him to ask her what was wrong, maybe suggest they meet to talk about things, but she wasn't prepared for his anger.

"I got your message," he said, almost before the word hello had left her mouth. "Thanks for that, Zoe. I'm dealing with all this crap and them when I get a spare few seconds and listen to my voicemail, I discover I've been dumped, too. Nice way to treat someone that only ever treated you with respect."

"I'm sorry . . ." began Zoe.

"Well, I just wanted you to know, you're off the hook. I won't bother you again. I don't need to force people into dating me, Zoe. If I haven't done enough by now to prove that I like you and that I'm serious, then there's no hope for the future anyway. So goodbye, and good luck with getting rid of that chip on your shoulder!"

And he was gone, leaving Zoe open-mouthed, phone still pointlessly clutched to her ear.

The next morning, Zoe tried to be positive. Today would be that new start she had promised herself after things had finished with Doug. No more pining after gorgeous hoteliers—she was going to move on with her life and start putting herself first.

Her attempt to convince herself she felt great was soon hampered when she opened her laptop and clicked onto her emails. The first message was from Rose Latimer, the woman she reported to at the website. In a few crisp lines, the woman for whom she had been freelancing for the past three years told her that budgets had been cut and unfortunately they would not be able to use her services anymore.

Zoe stared at the offending message for a few seconds.

Is this serious?

She thought about emailing back, letting Rose know how upset and offended she was by the terse nature of her message, that she deserved more after three years loyal service.

But she forced herself to walk away from the laptop and make herself a coffee. Life really knew how to slap a person in the face, didn't it? At times like this it would be really handy to have a multi-millionaire boyfriend to fall back on.

Zoe scolded herself for thinking like that and sat down on the sofa with her coffee, giving her panic time to subside.

What was she going to do? She needed to be practical, work out how long she had before she ran out of money. She had a few thousand in savings and she could always apply for a mortgage holiday for a few months. Maybe this was another positive dressed up like a negative. She'd wanted a fresh start, and now she could have one on a personal and professional level.

Her mobile phone burst into life. She picked it up from where it lay on the arm of the sofa, wondering if it would be Rose calling to apologise, but it was Michael. She considered not answering. The last thing she needed right now was another berating from him. But she accepted the call.

"Hi, Michael, this isn't the best time."

"I just called to say I think you're a fool."

Thanks, that's just what I need to hear right now.

"Just because you have this hang-up about us being from different worlds, you've ended something before it even had a chance to take off," Michael continued.

"I know!" snapped Zoe. "I know I'm an idiot. I know I have a chip on my shoulder, and I realise I panic too much—about everything! But right now, I need to think about what I'm going to do about work, because my long-term freelance client has just told me I'm surplus to requirements, and unlike you, I don't have a family business to fall back on. So, if you wanted me to suffer, you've got your wish. I'm sorry for finishing things by voicemail, it was a nasty and cowardly thing to do, but karma has well and truly caught up with me."

Zoe waited for Michael to respond, but he was silent.

"Hello?" She thought he might have hung-up.

"I'm still here," he said. "Why the hell would I want you to suffer?"

"For finishing with you."

"Zoe, I'm not sixteen years-old, I'm thirty-five. I'm an adult. I can deal with a bit of rejection. I was more angry at you for ending what we had—or what we could have had—because of some misguided idea that you weren't good enough for me."

"I never said that!" exclaimed Zoe, flushing with anger.

"Well, that's how you come across, Anyway, like I said, I'm not going to try and convince you to change your mind. I don't beg women to be with me. Although I do have a proposition for you?"

"What kind of proposition?"

"A professional one."

Where is this going? "Go on," she said cautiously.

"I'm looking to hire someone to do my personal PR. I've been undermined too much recently, and I want to build my public profile, make sure the industry and the business world knows that I'm good at what I do. Silence a few doubters."

"Right," said Zoe. "Where do I fit into to this?"

"You have experience in PR, don't you? And you've been a journalist and content writer. You could handle a position like this, right?"

"Well yes, I guess, but . . ."

"But what? We aren't romantically involved anymore, you saw to that, so why can't you work for me? I can be professional if you can. You need a job and I need a person with your skills. How about it?"

"Michael, this is madness. You could afford to take on someone with far more experience than me," said Zoe. "You don't have to offer me a job because you feel sorry for me. I'll be fine."

"Jesus Christ!" exclaimed Michael. "Here you go again!

Telling yourself and anyone who'll listen that you're not good enough. Just for once, take the bull by the horns, Zoe, and say yes to an opportunity."

Zoe felt the familiar panic surge through her. She needed time to think.

"Can I give you an answer tomorrow?"

"Sure. But don't leave it any longer. I want someone to start as soon as possible."

He didn't even say goodbye. The line was suddenly just dead. Zoe figured this was the side of Michael she would need to get used to if she took him up on his offer. No more Mr. Romantic. She would be dealing with Michael the CEO.

But was she seriously going to consider his offer? Could she really go from being romantically involved with him to being his personal PR, having him bark orders at her on a daily basis?

I need the money. Not that he even mentioned money, but I bet he won't be mean when it comes to a salary.

She spent the rest of the day and a restless night pondering Michael's offer and her other options. When she finally slept, it was to dream relentlessly of Michael. One moment he would be standing behind his desk, suited and booted, the next they would be naked in bed together, his glare boring into her soul, his strong arms wrapped around her, holding her in a vice-like grip as he pushed himself inside her.

She awoke to a rainy, bleak day, flushed and hot from her fantasies. She knew it was madness, but she also knew she didn't want to live without Michael in her life. She'd blown any chance of having a romantic relationship with him, but maybe she could make this work. She called him at 10 AM.

"If you were serious," she said as soon as he answered, "I'm interested. Why don't I come to your office and we can talk about how it will work?"

Chapter Seven

"I need you to come with me to Paris," said Michael during their daily briefing.

Zoe had been working with him for two weeks now, and so far it was proving just about bearable. For the first few days, she had found his new demeanour hard to take. There was no hint of the softness he had shown during their brief romance. He was every inch the high-flying businessman and she was very much his employee. He wasn't unpleasant with her, just officious. She was also desperately trying to train her brain not to picture him naked every time she saw him dressed in his designer suit. It was too easy for her mind to wander and imagine him walking around his desk and pulling her to him, the pair of them frantically stripping between fevered kisses. Both naked, Michael would press her against the floor-to-ceiling window of his office and push himself inside her, pulling her legs around his waist so that he could penetrate deep.

"Zoe, did you hear what I just said?" Michael was staring at her intently.

"Yes," she said. "You need me to come to Paris. But you don't have a hotel there do you?"

"Not yet, but premises have come onto the market that I want to look at."

"Don't you have people to do that for you?"

Michael stood and looked down at her with a condescending air. "Do I look like my surname is Hilton?" he asked, brusquely. "This is still a family company, and I have to actually work for a living. Yes, I have people who scout locations for me, and it's been brought to my attention that this could be a great site for a Britton Hotel."

Zoe's face was burning.

Michael turned to stare out of the window. Despite her anger, Zoe took the opportunity to admire his broad shoulders and narrow waist, that perfect bottom just visible beneath the hem of his suit jacket.

"I want you with me, as I want you to organise a one-to-one interview with Corporation Magazine while we're there. It's the leading French business journal. You can use the fact that I'm looking for expansion opportunities in France to get them interested. We're leaving next Monday, which gives you a week to get it all arranged."

"No problem," said Zoe, although her heart was palpitating at the thought of having to organise things so quickly. At least she spoke basic French.

"Okay," said Michael, still looking out of the window. "That's everything. Gill will let you know times of flights etcetera."

Gill was Michael's PA, a middle-aged harridan who thought the sun shone out of Michael's admittedly gorgeous backside.

With the feeling of rejection she now felt on a daily basis, Zoe left Michael's office and headed the short distance down the corridor to her own desk.

The headquarters of Britton Hotels were set in a low-rise, modern block in St James's, a very upmarket part of central London, a short walk from Piccadilly, with stunning views of St James's Park. Zoe's small office at least had that to offer, and she was grateful to have her privacy, rather than being forced to work in the open-plan space that many of the team members operated from.

"Hello, you must be Zoe."

Zoe looked up from her computer. A tall strikingly handsome man stood just inside her office door. It took her a moment to see the resemblance to Michael, but like an optical illusion, once she'd seen it, she couldn't un-see it. So, this must be the infamous Samuel. While the family resemblance was clear, his hair was straighter and lighter in colour than Michael's and his eyes were a steely grey rather than a mesmerizing blue. He filled a suit just as attractively though.

"Hi," said Zoe, standing and holding out her hand. "You must be Samuel."

"Oh dear." Samuel shook her hand and grinned. "My reputation proceeds me."

"Not at all. Well, not in a bad way."

"It's okay," said Samuel, still smiling. "I knew that you and Michael were briefly involved. Lucy filled me in. So I'm guessing he told you about our recent awkwardness. I'm hoping we can all be professional about it."

"Of course. That's something I've learned to do quite well over the past two weeks. Would you like to sit down?"

"No, no, I won't stay," replied Samuel. "I just wanted to say hello. I would have popped up sooner, but I've been in Paris."

"Really?" Alarm bells sounded in Zoe's head.

"Yes, Dad asked me to fly out and look at a site that's become available. Sadly, it wasn't right for us, but always worth checking these things out. Anyway, welcome onboard."

Samuel left her office, striding purposefully toward the elevators at the end of the corridor.

Should she tell Michael that Samuel was one step ahead of him where Paris was concerned?

She couldn't not tell him, but she didn't relish being the one to deliver the news.

"That bastard!" Michael slammed both fists down on his

desk, causing everything to vibrate violently. Zoe felt both alarmed and strangely aroused at seeing Michael in this state, his eyes blazing with anger, his whole body taut with aggression.

"I thought you'd want to know," said Zoe. "I'm guessing the Paris trip is off."

"No," snapped Michael. "The Paris trip is very much on. *I'll* decide if the property is right for us, not the bloody marketing director. What is my father playing at?"

"Maybe you should call him and find out," suggested Zoe.

Michael glared at her. "Why, thank you for that enlightened idea, Miss Harrison, how did I ever cope without you?"

Zoe hated herself for crying, but the tears were springing from her eyes before she had a chance to turn away. She rushed from Michael's office, managing to stifle her sobs until she'd closed her own office door behind her.

She couldn't cope with this. Working for him, having him speak to her like that after what they'd shared, it was all too much. She sat at her desk and brought up a blank document. She'd only been here two weeks. She hadn't even signed a contract yet. She'd write her resignation and just go.

"I'm sorry."

Startled, Zoe looked up. Michael was standing in front of her desk. She'd been so intent on what she was doing she hadn't even noticed his arrival. She tried to hold it together, but the tears came again.

"I can't do it," she sobbed. "I thought I could, but I can't."

And suddenly he was pulling her from her chair, and she was in his arms. He kissed her and she opened her mouth and welcomed his tongue. Michael thrust his hips forward, and she felt how hard he was. His hands were exploring, one stroking the back of her neck the other straying down to her bottom, pulling her even closer to his hardness. Her own hands explored, too, one resting on the taut muscles of his back, the other on his chest, which was solid and tight. She imagined dropping to her knees, unzipping his fly and taking him in her mouth, tasting him, getting pleasure from pleasing him, hearing his soft moans growing louder and more urgent. She'd never longed so much to pleasure a man before, but with Michael, there was the certainty that he would do the same for her.

"Wait!" Zoe pulled away.

"What's wrong?" he asked, the gaze from his dark-blue eyes fixed on her face.

"It's just . . ."

Michael released her and took a step backward. "Is this not what you want?" he asked.

"Yes, but I also need a job, and I know I can't have both. I also know I can't carry on the way we have been."

"Why can't you have both? We can see each other and still be professional when it comes to work."

"I'm so confused. I don't know what I want."

"Go home," said Michael. "Have the rest of the day off to think about everything. But if you want to keep your job and start dating again, I'm willing to give it a try."

Zoe took a deep breath and wiped the tears from her face with the back of her hand.

"Okay," she said, grabbing her coat and bag from the back of her chair. "I'll speak to you tomorrow."

She headed to the elevator in a daze, hoping she wouldn't bump into anyone on her way out.

The next morning she went straight to Michael's office and knocked on the door.

"Come in," called Michael's deep, rich voice.

Zoe pushed open the door, feeling strangely shy.

"Hi," Michael greeted. He was perched on the edge of his desk rather than behind it and was wearing a dark grey suit and a crisp white shirt, the top two buttons undone to reveal just a hint of his chest. Zoe felt the familiar rush of desire that swept through her whenever she was in Michael's presence.

"So?" he asked with a half-smile. "Is it good news or bad?"

"Good, I think," said Zoe, pushing the door closed behind her and stepping closer to him. "I want to keep my job. I want to prove to you and to myself that I can do it and do it well."

"I've never doubted that you could," said Michael, brow furrowed as he gazed at her with soulful-looking eyes.

"And I would also like to see where we can go—romantically, I mean."

Michael shifted his position, as if planning to stand.

"But," said Zoe, who had rehearsed this speech several times during the night. "Can we put that on hold until after Paris? I want to focus on doing that right, on being your personal PR and getting you some great coverage, without the distraction of there being an us. Does that make sense?"

"I guess." Michael didn't sound convinced.

"After Paris, I'd love to start again. We can go on a normal date, have a few glasses of wine and get flirty with each other. You don't need to create restaurants on roofs or fly me to a glamorous location, I just want to spend time with you and get to know you."

Michael appeared to ponder the suggestion, then he stood and held out his hand. "It's a deal."

Zoe shook the proffered hand, but before she could release it, Michael pulled her toward him.

"Can we at least enjoy a long kiss before the arrangement kicks in?" he asked, his firm chest pressed to hers, one hand flat against the small of her back, the other still clasping her own hand. His lips were just inches from hers, his warm breath caressing her cheek.

The door opened behind them and someone coughed.

"Samuel," sighed Michael, breaking the clinch and

stepping to one side.

Zoe spun round to see Michael's brother standing inside the doorway, smirking.

"How sweet," he said. "So the little romance is back on. How long did you manage to keep your hands off each other? Or has this been going on since Zoe started?"

"None of your business," said Michael, his voice icy cold.

"I wonder how Father would feel about you spending company money on your girlfriend, just to boost your own ego," said Samuel, leaning against the door frame, arms folded.

"I'm not spending the company's money," said Michael, "I'm paying Zoe out of my own finances, so no need to go running to Daddy. Talking of Father, I spoke to him yesterday about Paris. He said you told him I'd asked you to go and check out the premises. He also said you'd begged him to go to LA, he said you'd put it to him that you wanted to support me."

Samuel laughed. "Is that what he told you? Well, you believe that if it makes you feel better."

Samuel shifted his gaze to Zoe, who was still processing the information that Michael was paying her out of his own pocket. "I hope you're good at your job," he said, "because he certainly needs some positive PR."

"Oh, I'm good," replied Zoe, shocked at how confident she sounded. "But please don't ask me to do your personal PR, Samuel, because even I'm not that good."

And with that she marched toward the door. Samuel stepped to one side to let her pass, eyebrows raised in an expression of surprise.

Zoe had been polite with Samuel the first time she'd met him because she'd thought he was her superior within the company, but now that she knew she wasn't employed by Britton Hotels, she realised she didn't need to charm him.

Despite this, her heart was still pounding as she reached her own office. She stood for a moment with her back to the door, taking deep breaths.

It feels good to stand up to a bully like him, she thought.

Ten minutes later her phone bleeped. It was a message from Michael.

Well that told him!

Zoe smiled, but didn't reply. She had work to do.

Chapter Eight

Paris after dark was a beautiful sight, and from the bar on the 18th floor of their hotel, Zoe could see the city in all its splendour. More than any other city, Paris looked magical, like a painting by some great master, or a stunning piece of animation. Close by, the *arc de triomphe* stood like a sentinel over the Champs-Elysées, and beyond that the Eiffel Tower was currently twinkling like a Christmas Tree, much to Zoe's delight.

"What time are we meeting the journalist tomorrow?" asked Michael, who was perched on a bar stool next to her, less enthralled than she was by the glittering tower.

"Two o'clock," replied Zoe. "We're meeting her here. I thought that was better than booking somewhere near the property, just in case she worked out where the site was. I thought you might want that kept confidential."

Michael nodded. "Good thinking."

"Thanks, Boss."

"What's her name again?"

"Juliet Couture."

"Sounds sexy."

"I imagine she'll be very dull and middle-aged."

"As long as she writes good things about me, I don't care what she looks like."

"You'll have to make sure you say lots of intelligent stuff then, won't you?"

Michael sipped his Champagne. "Is she bringing a photographer?"

"Yes. So wear your blue suit, it brings out your eyes."

"Does it, now?" Michael smiled and held her gaze until she blushed.

Zoe glanced at the clock behind the bar. "Right, bedtime for me. Shall we meet at eight o'clock for breakfast?"

"Make it nine," said Michael. "I'll have a car pick us up at ten."

"Fine," said Zoe. "Well, goodnight."

She resisted the urge to kiss Michael on the cheek. She was the one who'd asked to keep things professional until this trip was over, after all.

"Good night, Zoe," Michael called after her. She still loved hearing him say her name.

When she got to her room, Zoe stripped and stepped into the walk-in shower. As the warm jets of water pleasantly pelted her skin, she thought of Michael. She imagined him naked stepping into the shower with her. She had seen nearly all of his beautiful body. There was only one part she had to create in her mind, and she took this part in her hand now, caressing it as they kissed. She imagined its length and thickness and how eventually it would feel as it slipped inside her. It all seemed so real—she could feel his stubbled cheek rub against hers, his lips brushing against her lips, his strong muscular arms pulling her closer.

The fantasy was so vivid, she was only vaguely aware of her hand stroking down her stomach and reaching between her legs.

She moaned his name as she imagined kissing him and pictured her hand teasing him. In her mind, it was his finger that gently pushed inside her, his finger that teased with tentative strokes, then sent tingling pleasure through her body as it worked with expert precision.

Zoe gasped with pleasure as orgasm swept over her. She looked upward so that the water splashed against her face.

Soon she wouldn't have to imagine anymore. She couldn't wait for that day to arrive.

"Juliet is meeting us in reception," Zoey said as they rode back from viewing the vacant hotel. "She's not bringing a photographer after all, she wants me to arrange to have some shots taken in your office when we get back."

"No problem," said Michael, who was checking emails on his phone.

"What did you think of the property?" asked Zoe.

Michael sighed. "I hate to admit it, but Samuel was right, I don't think it's for us. It's a beautiful building, but it would need completely gutting, plus that district just doesn't attract the tourist trade like it used to."

"We don't have to tell Juliet that, though. As far as she's concerned you're still interested in expanding into Paris if the right building becomes available."

"Absolutely," agreed Michael and as he spoke he opened his legs so that his right knee rested against Zoe's thigh.

Zoe didn't react. She didn't want to make a big thing of it, but she also wasn't going to encourage physical contact at this stage. She wanted to wait until they were back in London, maybe in Michael's house, which she had yet to see, before they gave in to their passion again. She wanted to be free to take it all the way, rather than indulging in a series of lust-filled clinches that couldn't go anywhere.

As the car drew up outside the hotel, Zoe spotted a stunning-looking woman entering through the main revolving door. She was tall and slender, her skin a light brown, her lush black hair tumbling over her shoulders. She was wearing a fitted dark suit, with a skirt so short it barely covered her backside, but which showed off her incredibly long legs to perfection.

As they climbed out of the car and headed into the hotel,

Zoe wondered if Michael had noticed the beautiful woman.

She was sitting in the reception area as they passed though. Zoe asked at reception if anyone had asked for them, and the cute young man behind the desk pointed toward the stunning woman.

"That's Juliet Couture!" exclaimed Zoe.

Overhearing her name, the woman stood and walked toward Zoe.

"Hello," she said, "Are you Zoe Harrison?"

Her English was perfect, which came as a relief.

"Yes," said Zoe, hurrying to meet her and shake hands. "And this is Michael Britton."

Michael didn't even attempt to hide his delight that his interviewer was to be this gorgeous creature—his face was positively beaming as he shook her hand.

"Pleasure to meet you," said Juliet.

"The pleasure is absolutely all mine," said Michael, offering one of his dazzling smiles.

"I don't think so," said Juliet, also smiling and fluttering her ridiculously long eyelashes.

"Shall we head up to the suite?" Zoe hoped she didn't sound as irritated as she felt.

Zoe led the way to Michael's suite, where Juliet and Michael sat side by side on a sofa, Juliet placing a small digital recorder on a nearby coffee table. They were sitting very close to each other, Zoe noticed. She half-expected Michael to rest his knee against the journalist's thigh.

"I'll leave you two to chat," said Zoe. "I'll be just over here if either of you need anything." She nodded to a chair on the other side of the living area.

"I'd love a coffee please," said Juliet, without taking her gaze off of Michael.

"No problem," said Zoe.

As she busied herself at the coffee machine, Zoe listened to

Michael and Juliet fall into easy conversation. Zoe had to admit, Juliet knew how to do her job. While she was confident Michael wouldn't reveal anything he shouldn't, he was talking very openly, obviously buoyed by the flirtatious interviewing techniques of the journalist.

The interview lasted for just over an hour. Zoe thought she might have to step in to bring it to a close, but finally Juliet leaned forward and switched off her recorder.

"Thank you so much, Michael," she said in her seductive accent. "That was very enlightening. I could have talked for hours.'

"Me too," said Michael, also standing.

"We could always continue over dinner later," said Juliet.

Zoe almost leapt out of her chair. "We have to catch a train back to London in two hours. But if you did want to ask Mr. Britton any further questions, you can always drop me an email, and I can organise a chat by phone or Skype."

Juliet didn't acknowledge Zoe, but instead rested a hand on Michael's shoulder and leaned in to plant a kiss on each of his cheeks.

"Well, if you should be in Paris again any time soon, do look me up," she said, then strode toward the door. "Can you get me images for the end of next week?"

It took Zoe a moment to realise this question was aimed at her.

"Oh, yes, of course," she replied, following the journalist to the door, but Juliet was already in the corridor beyond and striding toward the elevators.

"Wow," said Zoe, when the other woman was out of earshot. "What a cow."

"I liked her," said Michael, sitting back on the sofa.

"You hid it well."

"Are you jealous of the pretty journalist, darling?"

"No!" snapped Zoe, making herself a coffee, not because

she actually wanted one, but because she wanted to distract herself from how annoyed she did actually feel.

"I was just being charming. I want her to write nice things about me."

"Maybe you should have taken her up on the invitation to dinner." Zoe tried to control the emotion in her voice.

"Not when the alternative is travelling back on the Eurostar train with you," said Michael. "And I'm assuming that once we get back to London, we are officially dating again."

Zoe immediately softened. Michael certainly knew how to say the right thing at the right time.

"It will be late when we get back," she said.

"You could come to mine for a nightcap."

Zoe kept her back to Michael so he wouldn't see the colour rising up her neck.

"Maybe another night this week," she said. "I would like to see where you live."

"Bring an overnight bag."

"Coffee?" asked Zoe, to change the subject, glancing at Michael over her shoulder.

He grinned. "Yes please, darling. And then we can check out and grab some lunch somewhere near Gare du Nord."

It hadn't escaped Zoe's notice that Michael had called her darling twice in the space of a few minutes. There was no way that could be a slip of the tongue. Warmth spread through her body as she wondered yet again what making love to Michael would be like.

As it turned out, Zoe would have to wait longer than expected to finally make love to Michael. The day after they returned from Paris, he was forced to fly to Rome to oversee a problem with the staff at the company's hotel in the city. Apparently there was a troublemaker in their midst who had convinced the entire team to come out on strike, demanding better working condition and pay. Michael had said on numerous occasions, and Zoe believed him, that the staff working for Britton Hotels were treated well and paid more than the going rate, so Zoe suspected foul play was once again at work.

Despite feeling despondent over Michael's absence, Zoe busied herself organizing a photographer to come to the offices the following week to take a series of images of Michael for the French magazine and for any other journals that might require a photo of her handsome boss.

She was in the process of emailing several journalists to gage their interest in interviewing Michael when someone knocked on her office door. She hadn't even said *come in* when the door opened, revealing Samuel. She was surprised to see him dressed in sports gear, a sweatshirt and jogging bottoms, plus a pair of no doubt very expensive trainers. She'd never seen him dressed in anything but a suit until now.

"Hello," said Zoe, her guard up immediately.

"Hi, Zoe," said Samuel cheerily. "I'm just on my way to the gym on the top floor."

"Good for you."

"But I thought I'd pop in and see how you were doing first."

Zoe couldn't help but notice how handsome Samuel was He didn't have the brooding good looks of Michael, but he was still striking, his cheek bones prominent, and the stare from those grey eyes seemed to pierce right into her brain and read her thoughts. He also suited the casual attire. It made him look younger and more fresh faced. He was only in his early thirties, after all. And he appeared not to be wearing any underwear, judging from the revealing outline that bulged through the material.

"I'm absolutely fine, why wouldn't I be?" replied Zoe, averting her eyes.

"I just thought you might be missing Michael, that's all. I was going to offer to take you to dinner."

"He only left this morning. And I really don't think dinner would be a good idea, do you?"

"Why not?" Samuel advanced into the office, perching one firm butt cheek on the edge of her desk. He did have a very appealing bottom. Zoe tried not to look at it, but it was hard to avoid while it rested just a few feet from her face.

"I'm really busy, Samuel."

"We don't have to be enemies, Zoe. There's no reason we can't be friends."

"Maybe when Michael gets back, we can go out as a foursome," said Zoe. "How is Lucy?"

"She's fine," said Samuel, dismissively. "When you say foursome, you're talking dinner or something, right?"

"Well, I'm certainly not suggesting we all have sex together!" exclaimed Zoe.

Samuel seemed to consider this prospect for a moment. "Leave Michael out of the equation, and that could work," he said.

Zoe grimaced, although she was actually feeling weirdly aroused by the conversation.

"Samuel, please, I need to get on, so unless you have something work-related to tell me . . ."

"Okay, okay," Samuel slipped off of her desk and walked to the door, giving her ample time to admire his cotton-clad backside. "But if you change your mind, you know where I am."

Zoe had a brief vision of Samuel under the shower following his workout, soaping up his muscular chest, hand slipping down to his crotch and lathering up his obviously ample member.

Stop it!

She hoped Michael would sort out the problem in Rome and be back before the end of the week. She really needed to have sex, and soon.

CHAPTER NINE

Of course, it wasn't just sex Zoe wanted from Michael—she wanted a relationship. It might be early days, but she already knew she wanted to be with him. Making love would just be her way of expressing those feelings, and she thought he felt the same way. Although knowing herself and her tendency to overthink everything, she'd probably be doubting Michael's intentions within a day or so.

As she sank into a warm bath that evening, feeling satisfied after a successful day at work, Zoe focused on everything that was good in her life. Her flat, her new job, the blossoming romance with Michael. So much had changed in such a short space of time, but she wanted to enjoy the adventure and not worry about where it could all go wrong.

She was pulling on her bathrobe and thinking about treating herself to a chilled glass of wine, when the doorbell rang. Cursing, Zoe walked to the intercom next to the front door and pushed the communication button.

"Who is it?" she asked.

"It's me," came the deep male voice.

"Michael?"

Had he really travelled to Rome and back in a day?

The caller didn't respond, but she was sure she recognised his voice. She pressed to button that opened the main front door and hurried back to the bathroom to make sure she looked presentable, despite being dressed in a bathrobe. She hadn't planned for Michael to see her without make-up quite this early in their relationship, but she could hardly keep him waiting for half an hour while she beautified herself.

The caller tapped at the door to her apartment. Zoe pulled her bathrobe open a little at the neck so that the tops of her breasts were showing seductively and went to answer the knock.

"Hi," she greeted as she pulled the door open. But the word caught in her throat. It was Samuel standing on the landing, not Michael.

"Hello," he said, blatantly eyeing her cleavage.

Zoe hastily pulled the top of her robe closed. The fact that Samuel was, once again, suited and booted, made her feel even more exposed.

"What are you doing here?" she demanded. "How did you even know where I lived?"

"Michael's London driver is very easy to get information out of. Are you going to ask me in?"

"No, I just got out of the bath. It's not a good time. To be honest, Samuel, I don't think there will ever be a good time for you to visit my flat."

"Oh come on, Zoe, what's wrong with you? I just thought we could share a bottle of fizz together and talk about how I can mend this rift with Michael." As he spoke, he held of a bottle of Champagne which had been concealed behind his back.

"That's between you and Michael," insisted Zoe. "I'm not getting involved. Now please go, Samuel. I want to enjoy a quiet evening on my own."

"Seriously," said Samuel, raising one eyebrow. "You'd rather be on your own than spend an evening with me. I'm pretty good company, and I have everything Michael has. Actually, according to Lucy, I might have a fraction more. I saw you admiring it earlier."

"Samuel, what is this about?" asked Zoe, continuing to block his way into the flat.

"I was just offering an olive branch. But I can see I'm wasting my time."

"It's Michael you seem to have a problem with, not me."

Samuel sighed and ran a hand through his light brown hair, briefly sweeping the fringe back from his high forehead. "I was hoping you could help me mend the rift. But I obviously got that wrong."

"Maybe if you stopped stealing his girlfriends and constantly trying to undermine him at work, the rift would mend itself," suggested Zoe.

Samuel laughed, but it was a joyless sound. "Is that what you think this is?" he said, with scorn. "You seriously think I'm here to try and steal you from Michael. Believe me, Zoe, you don't interest me at all. No one understands what Michael sees in you, apart from the fact that you're the complete opposite of Lucy."

Zoe felt like he'd physically punched her in the gut. Even though she knew he was deliberately trying to hurt her, she couldn't help but feel the sting of his words.

"Just go." She made to slam the door, but Samuel blocked it with his foot.

"I'll go when I'm ready to go.

Zoe was genuinely scared. She'd thought Samuel was creepy, but now he was coming across as unhinged. She considered shouting for help, asking one of the neighbours to call the police.

Samuel stared at her and Zoe stared back, refusing to show that she felt intimidated.

"You really are pathetic," he said eventually and removed his foot from between the door and its frame.

"I think you win the title of *World's Most Pathetic Person* right now," replied Zoe, as she pushed the door closed.

She waited, breathing heavily, listening to the sound of his footsteps on the stairs and the main front door slamming shut.

She hurried over to a window and saw him climbing into a red Porsche. He revved up the engine so that the roar brought several people to their windows, then sped off at a dangerous speed.

Zoe sat on the sofa, heart pounding. Should she call Michael and tell him? No, he had enough to worry about without bothering him with this nasty little episode. She'd wait until he got back from Rome and tell him face to face.

She decided to pour herself the glass of wine she'd promised herself earlier. As she held the glass to her lips, she realised her hand was shaking. She wasn't sure Samuel would give in so easily next time.

Zoe felt nervous going into work the next day. Her heart was beating more rapidly than normal as she stepped out of the elevator and walked towards her office. She had no idea how to react if she bumped into Samuel, or whether he'd have the nerve to come to her office. His behaviour had been appalling—totally unacceptable—but he was also a senior director within the company, and she had no doubt he could twist the truth to suit him. With this in mind, she had already decided not to have any confrontations with him in front of other people. If he did come to her office, she would have a thing or two to say, however. How dare he come to her home and act like that? Her flat was her refuge from the world, and he had no right to violate that.

Someone knocked on her office door. Zoe stiffened. But when the door was opened and she saw that Michael was her visitor, her agitation evaporated and she stood, smiling.

"You're back," she said, walking around her desk to meet him. They hugged and he felt warm and strong.

"Is that any way to greet your boss?" asked Michael, kissing her firmly on the lips.

"Oh, shut up. For the next ten minutes you're my lover, not

my boss."

Michael looked at his watch and frowned. "I usually like to take a bit longer than ten minutes, but if that's all you have to offer . . ." He began to loosen his tie.

Zoe laughed and gave his arm an affectionate slap before returning to her seat. Michael took the chair the other side of her desk.

"So, what happened in Rome?" asked Zoe, "Did you get to the bottom of it?"

"Yes and no. I managed to calm the situation. I spoke to all the employees and asked then to be open about what they were unhappy about. It turned out most of them didn't really understand why they had gone on strike. One name kept cropping up – Dennis Archer, an English guy who joined the team a few months ago as an assistant chef. He seems to have been the ringleader, but he disappeared the day I arrived. Everyone seemed a bit vague on how he was hired in the first place. But it seems likely he was a plant."

"Working for one of your competitors?"

"I guess so."

"And do you think all the incidents around the world are connected?"

Michael shrugged. "I'd say yes, but we don't actually have a competitor in each location. I mean the major chains operate there, but I can't imagine them losing sleep over us."

"Yes that is strange."

"Anyway, I didn't come here to talk about Rome. I came to whisk you away from all this."

"But I have work to do," protested Zoe.

"Bring your laptop with you," said Michael, standing.

"Where are we going?" asked Zoe, feeling flustered.

"My parents are away in France at the moment, and they have said I can use their house in Cornwall if I want to."

"I can't just go to Cornwall! I don't have a change of clothes with me."

"We'll stop at yours on the way. Just throw a few things into a bag. We'll only be there a couple of nights. You'll love it. It has amazing views of the sea. Plus they always have loads of food stored in the freezers."

Zoe laughed. "Okay," she relented. "Give me ten minutes to send out a few urgent emails and I'll be with you."

Zoe was already trying to remember what sexy underwear she had washed and ready to wear. Michael wasn't taking her to the Cornish coast for some sea air. This was it, the night they would finally make love, and she wanted to look her best.

Michael drove them to Cornwall in a cute convertible. Despite it being October, it was a warm day and not too windy, so they kept the roof down for much of the journey. Within five hours they were driving down winding country lanes with towering hedgerows, the occasional break in the foliage offering incredible rural views. Michael's parents' house was situated a little way along the coast from St Ives, a pretty seaside town that Zoe had visited several times with her family as a child. She caught a brief glimpse of the port and the frothing sea before they continued along the road that would take them to their destination.

Zoe had built up a picture in her mind of what the Britton family home would look like, but her vision of a sprawling Gothic manor house could not have been further from the reality.

"Here we are," announced Michael, turning a sharp bend at the end of a long dirt track.

"Wow!" Zoe gasped, staring at the ultra-modern extensively glass building before them. It was as big as she'd imagined, rising four stories, with seemingly random geometrically shaped extensions jutting out from every side. One cube-shaped room actually seemed to hang out over the cliff edge. Zoe wasn't sure how secure she would feel standing in that part of the house.

"It's incredible," she said, transfixed by the contemporary splendour of it. "It's not what I expected at all."

"My parents are very cool for old people. They had this built a few years back. Before that, they lived in a Georgian property, set in several acres, but it was constantly in need of renovation, and they didn't want the hassle. So they built their dream house in the perfect spot, and they intend to live out their days here, watching the waves crash against the shore."

"You make it sound very romantic." Zoe climbed out of the car, gaze still fixed on the stunning property.

Michael led the way up a flight of sturdy wooden steps to a large decking area. Already the views of the deserted beach and endless ocean were incredible. Zoe couldn't wait to see what they were like from the top floor.

Michael took her hand and led her to the front door. He swiped an electronic key across a panel and then, following a positive-sounding bleep, entered a five-digit password.

Once inside the vast hallway, Michael entered another code into a panel just inside the door, presumably an alarm system.

"There," he said. "Welcome to Cliff View, home to my illustrious parents.

"It is truly breath taking," said Zoe, turning a full circle in order to take in the splendour of the entrance hall. It was an immense space of white and glass. A stairway to the left led up to a mezzanine level, and on either side, shorter flights of stairs led through vast entranceways to more rooms, with gorgeous views, either of the sea or of sprawling countryside.

"Shall we take our bags upstairs, and then I'll give you a proper tour?" Michael headed toward the back of the hallway and turned right.

Zoe followed him and found herself in a corridor, with more rooms off to the left hand-side and a wide set of stairs straight ahead.

"The bedrooms are all on the third and fourth floors. Would you like a view of the sea or of rolling fields?"

"I'd like the exact same view as you. When Michael turned to look at her, she offered him a knowing smile.

"Sea view it is," said Michael, leading the way up the stairs.

They ate a late lunch on the terrace leading from the bedroom. It was a simple meal of cold meats and cheeses, washed down with a crisp Sauvignon Blanc. Their food finished, they remained at the white wooden table, sipping wine and gazing out across the sea. A gust of wind blew across the terrace and Zoe shivered.

"Cold?" asked Michael.

"A little."

"Do you want to go inside?"

"Maybe."

Michael stood and held out his hand to her, as if proposing they dance. When Zoe took it, he pulled her to her feet and then to his chest, pressing his lips to hers.

Zoe melted into the embrace. She could hear waves crashing against the rocks below, but mostly she was aware of Michael's warm body pressed to hers, of his growing hardness and the touch of his full lips.

He unfastened the first four buttons of her blouse and slipped a hand underneath, stroking her breast through her bra. His other hand stroked down her side to her stomach, resting there teasingly for a moment, before slipping down a little further. Zoe gasped and rested her hand on his, directing it, as she lifted her short skirt. His fingers probed beneath her panties, where she was already moist, ready for him.

They began to edge backward into the bedroom, maintaining their embrace, his finger finding her pleasure spot so that she tingled all over.

She unzipped the fly of his tailored trousers, slipping a hand inside and gripping his hardness through the cotton of his briefs. He was as big as she'd imagined. Even through the cotton she could feel the network of bulging veins, the curve of his swollen glans. Desperate to feel him inside her, she fell back on the bed.

Michael unzipped her skirt and tugged it off. She removed her blouse and threw it onto the floor. She was glad she'd changed into some fancy underwear. She made to kick off her stiletto shoes, but Michael shook his head.

"Leave them on for now," he said.

Zoe shuddered with desire as Michael removed his shirt, revealing his perfectly toned chest and stomach. Next he unbuttoned his trousers and pushed them down to his ankles. At some point he must have kicked his own shoes off, as he was able to step out of his trousers so that he stood at the end of the bed in just his briefs and socks. Hs white underpants were bulging with his hard member, its shape and size clearly visible through the stretched cotton.

Michael gripped the hem of his briefs and pushed them slowly down.

The bedroom door opened.

"Jesus!" Michael grabbed his trousers from the floor and held them against himself to cover his arousal.

Zoe stared at the blonde woman who had stepped into the room and now stood with her mouth wide open, staring in shocked disbelief first at Michael and then at Zoe.

It was Lucy.

"What's wrong?" came a deep male voice from behind her and now Samuel stepped into the room.

Zoe grabbed for the side of the quilt and pulled it over her almost naked body, but not before Samuel's steely gaze had scanned every inch of her.

"What are you doing here?" demanded Michael.

"I was going to ask you the same thing," said Samuel. "Well, I guess it's pretty clear what you're doing."

"Get out!" shouted Michael.

Samuel raised his hands in a gesture of submission and backed out of the room, Lucy followed him, looking suitably mortified.

Once they had closed the door behind them, Michael threw his trousers back on the floor and swore loudly. He was no longer hard.

"I can't believe this," he fumed.

Zoe stared at his beautiful naked body and felt like crying.

"I'm guessing your parents offered Samuel and Lucy the house for a couple of nights, too," she said. "We should get dressed and go talk to them. The longer we leave it, the more awkward it will be."

CHAPTER TEN

The wonderful tranquillity of the house of glass by the ocean had been obliterated by the arrival of Samuel and Lucy. Michael seemed ready to self-combust as he sat brooding at the wide oak dining table that filled much of the kitchen. Zoe sat next to him, with Lucy and Samuel sitting across from them. Lucy had made a cafetiere of coffee, as if to try and bring some normality to the situation.

"I'm sorry we've ruined your night away," she said. "We obviously had no idea you were going to be here. Your father suggested we come, and he didn't say anything about having said the same to you. Maybe he was deliberately trying to bring you guys together."

Zoe couldn't help but notice that Lucy seemed like a much softer version of herself. She wasn't the cold power-dresser she had met in LA She actually looked quite vulnerable dressed in a simple roll-neck sweater and jeans, holding her mug of coffee in both hands.

"How are we going to make this work?" asked Samuel, "Because there's no way I'm driving all the way back to London tonight."

"There'll be hotels in St Ives," said Michael.

"Surely this place is big enough for the four of us to co-exist for a couple of days. We work together for God's sake," said Samuel.

Zoe was glad she hadn't mentioned Samuel's visit to her flat during the drive to the house. The tension was palpable enough without that adding to it.

Michael looked at Zoe. "Do you feel up to another five-hour drive today?" he asked.

Zoe shook her head. "Samuel's right," she said, although she hated to agree with the arrogant man. "This place is huge. We don't even have to see each other again if we don't want to. Surely we can agree just to stick to our own parts of the house."

Michael blew through his full lips and sighed. "So much for getting away from it all."

"I'm sorry," said Lucy. "I realise it can't be easy seeing Samuel and me together like this but . . ."

Michael glared at her. "Seeing you and Samuel together doesn't bother me at all," he said. "I've not given you a second thought in the past month. I just wanted two nights away from London and work and any reminder of work. Your presence here really doesn't affect me one way or another."

Lucy's mouth trembled and she stood, covering her face with a hand, and hastened from the room.

"That was harsh," said Samuel.

"Do you think I care?" Michael's icy tone suggested that he really didn't.

"Fine," said Samuel. "We'll take a bedroom on the third floor on the other side of the house. There's a small kitchen up there, too, so we'll stock up the fridge so we don't even have to come down here for food or wine. Satisfied?"

"I guess I'll have to be," said Michael.

Samuel nodded and stood. He looked very tall and imposing in his grey suit, his white shirt pulled tight by his expansive chest.

"I hope you guys have a fun couple of days," he said. "You certainly look very well, Zoe."

He left before either Zoe or Michael could react, but as the door closed behind him Michael flung his empty coffee mug across the kitchen. It hit a wall and shattered.

"Michael, don't let him get to you." said Zoe, shaken by the outburst.

Michael was breathing heavily and glaring into space.

"I'm sorry," he said finally. "I just hate that man sometimes. I could break his neck right now and not feel any remorse."

"You don't mean that."

Michael's hypnotic gaze rested on hers. "Don't I?"

They returned to their bedroom, although the unexpected interruption had obviously quelled Michael's passion. Zoe, on the other hand, felt strangely aroused by having been seen by Michael's brother and ex-girlfriend. At first, she'd been embarrassed, but now the memory of lying on the bed—dressed only in underwear and a pair of stiletto shoes, damp and ready for Michael while Samuel gawped at her—was making her heart pound, and her desire for Michael was more intense than ever.

Michael walked out onto the terrace and leaned on the rail, staring moodily out to sea like a captain pining for the ocean. Zoe followed him, placing a hand on his shoulder.

"I'm sorry," Michael said, still gazing toward the horizon. "I wanted this to be special, and that bastard has ruined it."

"Not if we don't let him. The sun is about to set, and we are in a beautiful location with views to die for."

"I know I shouldn't let him get to me." Michael turned to face her, his blue eyes like beacons in the dusk. "But he seems to want to either destroy or steal everything I have. He's been the same since we were kids. But lately it seems to have reached a whole new level."

"It does sound like turning up here at the same time as us was an accident. Perhaps Lucy is right, and your parents were hoping they could force you and Samuel to spend some time together away from the business."

"I don't want to spend time with him. I don't like him. Why do I need to like him, just because he's my brother?"

Zoe began to stroke Michael's back, was hoping the contact might ignite something again. She couldn't forget the image of him standing at the end of the bed, hard as iron, about to climb on top of her, about to enter her, fill her.

Her hand slipped down to his butt, resting there, soaking in the body heat.

"Are you coming on to me?" asked Michael, eyebrows raised.

"I might be." Zoe gave the firm cheek a gentle squeeze.

Suddenly Michael grabbed her and pulled her to him, kissing her neck and the top of her breasts, then her mouth, his tongue finding hers as his hands explored her body. Zoe pulled open his shirt, aware of at least two buttons flying across the terrace. She broke from the kiss in order to lick his hard nipples, flicking them with the tip of her tongue. Michael shrugged his shirt off,, then finished unbuttoning her blouse, exposing her bra, which he unhooked with expert speed, revealing her breasts. He pulled the blouse from her body and threw it on top of his shirt, then began caressing her breasts with his large, warm hands, tweaking the nipples until they were fully erect and seeming to sing with ecstasy.

They kissed with growing passion. Zoe felt her skirt drop to the ground and Michael's hand slip beneath the waistband of her knickers, his finger once again finding the centre of her pleasure. She cried out, arching her back, unzipping his fly and pulling open his trousers. She gripped his hardness in her hand, feeling it throb at her touch.

"I want you so much," she whispered.

With a shriek of delight, she found herself scooped from the floor and lying in Michael's arms. He stared down at her with his beautiful, intense eyes, then carried her to the bedroom.

Michael laid her on the bed, then stripped naked, his gaze never leaving her face. Zoe started to pull off her skirt, but he shook his head, leaning over her, his huge member standing solid and stiff between his toned thighs. taking hold of the hem, he slid her skirt down over her waist. Next he tugged down her panties, all the time holding her gaze. As he threw her knickers onto the floor, he kneeled on the bed, leaning in closer and kissing her stomach, then running his tongue over her bush.

Zoe arched her back, stroking herself between her legs to show him what she wanted. He shifted position, sliding a hand beneath her bottom and lying flat across the bed, kissing her smooth thighs, then tracing a line with his tongue up to where her own fingers were causing her to moan softly with pleasure. He kissed her there, too, until she removed her now moist fingers to make way for his tongue. She stifled a scream of ecstasy as he teased her clitoris, moaning appreciatively, his breath warm between her legs.

"I want you inside me!" whispered Zoe.

And finally, as dusk fell, with the sound of waves crashing on the shore, they made love. Zoe had never experienced pleasure like it. Michael felt so large inside her, but he managed to be both a forceful and gentle lover, ensuring each thrust of his manhood brought her as much enjoyment to her as it did him. For the first time ever she reached orgasm at the same time as her lover, screaming out in ecstasy as he too let out a roar of passion and satisfaction.

As they lay together in the dark afterward, Michael's arm wrapped around her, Zoe's head on his chest, listening to his pounding heart, no one else mattered, no one else existed. The night and the house were theirs and theirs alone.

When Zoe woke it was to hazy daylight. She glanced at the clock on the bedside table and saw that it was only seven o'clock. She couldn't remember what time she had fallen asleep, only that it was after making love with Michael for the third time. Michael was sleeping soundly beside her, so Zoe decided to go down to the kitchen and make them both coffee.

She pulled on her panties, which lay next to the bed and slipped on the silk dressing gown she had hung in the wardrobe when they arrived.

She felt contented and light as she headed downstairs and hummed happily to herself as she prepared coffee in the vast kitchen.

She was lost in her own thoughts when she felt a solid body press against her back and a hand rest on her buttocks through her robe. Smiling, she turned to greet Michael.

"Morning," said Samuel.

"What the . . ." Zoe leaped away from him, almost knocking the full cafetiere off of the counter.

Samuel was dressed in a short white bathrobe that fell to just above his knees. It was gaping open at the tops so that most of his wide chest was revealed.

He laughed and held his hands up, as he had before in the bedroom.

"Sorry, I was just messing with you!"

"Well, don't!" snapped Zoe. "That was totally inappropriate, I don't want you touching me—ever! Is that clear?"

"You seemed happy for me to look at you yesterday, while you lay on the bed in your sexy underwear," said Samuel, as he perused her body, his grey eyes filled with lust.

Zoe was aware that under the robe she was naked apart from her panties. She was shocked at the rush of arousal she suddenly felt, mixed with trepidation at what Samuel would say or do next.

"I wasn't expecting you," she said, moving a little further from Samuel, who immediately shifted forward so that she was almost pinned against the kitchen counter. She could smell his morning body odour, a musky, manly scent.

"Back off!" she barked. "Or I will scream this house down."

"Oh, get over yourself." Samuel, turned and headed over to the fridge. "I just came down for some fresh milk."

"And you thought you'd just molest me as a side project."

"Don't be such a drama queen. I was just having a joke with you."

Zoe stood fuming, waiting for Samuel to leave.

"See you later," he said, walking away. "Try and keep the noise down if you have morning sex. The sound of you screaming kept Lucy and me awake last night. It must have been loud for us to hear you in a house this size."

Zoe didn't respond. She had to say something to Michael before Samuel took things any further, but in this atmosphere, she was frightened he might seriously harm Samuel.

A buzzing sound drew her attention to the kitchen table and a mobile phone sitting on top of it. Presumable Samuel had put it down there in order to grope her and forgotten to take it with him. Zoe glanced at the name of the caller. It was Dennis Archer. Why did that name sound familiar? It took her a few moments to place it. It was the man who had stirred up trouble at the Rome hotel. Why would he be calling Samuel?

And then she realised exactly why the plant from Rome would be calling Samuel. She was pretty sure they'd find other plants in LA and London, people willing to carry out nasty little deeds in return for a nice tax-free payment from Samuel.

She pondered the best way to inform Michael of everything as she carried two cups of coffee back to the bedroom, but as soon as Michael, now sitting up in bed with a drowsy expression on his face, saw her, he knew something was wrong.

"Are you okay?" he asked as she placed his coffee on the bedside table nearest him.

Zoe tried to lie and say she was fine, but she didn't want to protect Samuel. He was a vile letch and probably a backstabbing brother and he deserved to be exposed.

"Not really," she admitted, sitting on the edge of the bed and placing her coffee next to Michael's as the cup and saucer were rattling in her shaking hand. "It's Samuel."

Michael sat bolt upright. "What has he done?"

"He came to my flat while you were in London and tried to convince me to let him in for a cosy chat."

"What?" Michael immediately flew into a rage.

"Wait," said Zoe. "I sent him away, obviously, and he said some pretty nasty things. And just now he tried it on with me in the kitchen. I dealt with it, but it wasn't pleasant. I'm only telling you because I don't want it to be a secret that he can somehow hold over me."

"I'll kill him," said Michael, throwing back the quilt, ready to jump out of bed and confront his brother.

"No, don't," insisted Zoe. "I think that's what he wants, to rile you to the point that you lose it."

"Well, it's worked," said Michael, climbing from the bed and searching the bedroom floor for some clothes. His bottom was slightly paler than the rest of his tanned body and his back and shoulders rippled with muscles. He really was perfection.

"Please, Michael. I don't want this. I need you to sit down and talk to me."

"I can't just let him get away with threatening you," fumed Michael. "This needs to end now."

"There's more.

Michael turned to face her, and Zoe had to catch her breath at how gorgeous he looked, naked and filled with rage, but also still drowsy.

"What?" snapped Michael. "Tell me."

"I think Samuel's behind all the scares that have been happening at the hotels."

Michael looked confused.

"He left his phone in the kitchen, and I saw he had a call from someone called Dennis Archer."

Michael repeated the name to himself and Zoe saw realisation dawn on his face. "Are you sure?"

"Totally."

"You think he organised all the problems that we've had over the past few weeks to try and undermine me?"

"It sounds crazy that he'd risk the family company like that," admitted Zoe. "But I think maybe Samuel *is* a little crazy."

"Right! That's it! He's history."

"Wait!" insisted Zoe. "If you barge straight in now and accuse him and punch his lights out, you'll play right into is hands. We need proof, more than a missed call on his mobile."

Michael stared at her, breathing heavily, then sat on the end of the bed next to her. "Okay," so how are we going to get this proof then?"

"Maybe I can help."

Chapter Eleven

"If you seriously don't want me to knock Samuel out, we need to leave now." Michael was pulling on his clothes as he spoke. "Because if I see that smug face of his, I'll be tempted to bloody kill him, Zoe."

"Okay, okay," said Zoe, also dressing, desperate to get Michael out of the house before there was a major incident.

They were packed within minutes, and Michael led the way downstairs to the hallway. Samuel was standing near the front door, holding a mug of coffee and looking pensive.

"Oh, hi," he said, glancing at them both, lifting his steaming mug as if in a toast. "I was just trying to decide which room to drink this in."

Michael dropped his bag and marched toward him.

"Michael, no!" screamed Zoe.

But Michael already had Samuel by the throat.

"How dare you touch Zoe!" he yelled, slamming Samuel against the nearest wall. the mug crashed to the floor, spattering the surrounding white with coffee.

"What's going on?" Lucy appeared on the stairs behind Zoe.

"I should kill you!" bellowed Michael, his face pressed just an inch from his brother's. "Touch her again, and I will."

Samuel managed to shove Michael backward—he was the bigger of the two, although Michael's rage seemed to have made him the stronger.

"What did she tell you?" asked Samuel, with a sneer. "That I came onto her? Why would I be interested in her when I already have Lucy?"

"Because you know I care for her, that's why!?" shouted Michael, fists clenched at his sides—for now.

"She was begging for some attention," said Samuel. "She's a little gold digger and she doesn't care which brother she gets it from."

Zoe heard the crunch of bone as Michael's fist made contact with Samuel's face. A spray of blood spattered across the wall behind him.

Zoe grabbed Michael's bag and ran toward front door. "Michael, please leave with me now before this gets out of hand."

Samuel was leaning against the wall, hand on his nose trying to stem the flow of blood.

"Tomorrow, I want your resignation on my desk," said Michael. "We don't employ sex offenders at Britton Hotels."

"That isn't going to happen," said Samuel. "It's my company as much as yours."

"Fine." Michael grabbed his bag from Zoe. "Let's see how your career flourishes with a charge of sexual assault against you."

Samuel laughed. "What proof do you have? Unless you've had CCTV installed in the kitchen."

"That sounded like a confession to me," said Zoe, pulling open the door. She glanced at Lucy, who stood on the far side of the hallway, white as a ghost.

"And you asked me why," continued Samuel. "Georgia, that's why. Have you told Zoe how you killed the love of my life?"

Michael stormed through the open door toward his car and Zoe followed.

Zoe gave Michael a few minutes to calm down before asking the unavoidable question.

"Michael, who was Georgia and what did Samuel mean?"

Michael visibly stiffened, barely avoiding a car coming down the narrow lane from the opposite direction. The driver of the other vehicle sounded his horn and mouthed something obscene, but Michael didn't react.

"It's not the way he makes it sound," he replied, still staring at the road ahead.

"Tell me. This is too big to just ignore."

"Okay," said Michael. Although he seemed calmer, there was still so much anger in his eyes. "Georgia was Samuel's first girlfriend, back when he was sixteen. Believe it or not, he was quite shy back then, not that confident around girls. But Georgia was a vivacious, loveable girl, and she really brought him out of himself. He became far more sociable and was actually a decent guy. We were close then . . ."

"So, what happened?"

"I'm trying to tell you," snapped Michael.

"Sorry," said Zoe. "Go on."

"The two of them were pretty much inseparable from day one of meeting," continued Michael. "Georgia and her family moved next door to the old family house in Fulham. My dad was still very much running the company then, so we spent most of our time in London, although we also had a country house in Cornwall."

"All right for some."

Michael ignored the interruption and continued. "It was the summer of 2002, and I was looking forward to going to university after the holidays. Although he was always with Georgia, Samuel was happy for the three of us to hang out. I was between girlfriends at the time. My previous love, Moya Belgradia, had ditched me for an older guy with a private island . . ."

Fulham, London, 2002

Michael hesitated on his way across the lawn. He could see Samuel and Georgia, and they appeared to be sharing an intimate moment, which he didn't want to interrupt.

They were sitting on the edge of the orchard that filled the end of the garden. Well, Samuel was sitting, Georgia was lying down, her head on Samuel's thigh, basking in the warmth of the late spring sun. Her voice carried across the garden, and Michael felt guilty for listening into their private conversation.

"Do you think we'll get married?" she asked.

"What?" Samuel put down the book he was reading and stared down at her. "We're sixteen!"

"I don't mean soon," said Georgia. "But one day."

Samuel pursed his lips, as if in deep thought. "Well, we've been seeing each other for three months, so I guess marriage is next on the agenda."

"Oh, shut up!" laughed Georgia. "I was just being stupid. Ignore me."

Samuel gave her hair an affectionate stroke. "I'd never ignore you.

"Give it a few years," said Georgia. "The novelty will wear off."

"Never," said Samuel. "Oh, here comes Michael."

Michael jolted at the mention of his name. He'd been spotted. He continued walking, trying to hide the fact that he'd been eavesdropping.

Georgia sat up and smiled at him. She was blushing. Maybe she realised Michael had overheard her immature question.

"Hey guys!" Michael greeted, crouching opposite them. "Am I interrupting a romantic moment?"

"No," said Georgia.

"I thought he was," said Samuel, although he was being good natured.

"Fancy a coming to see a film with me?" Michael asked.

"What were you thinking of watching?" asked Georgia.

"The Pianist is meant to be good. Or if you fancy something lighter, there's the new Bond movie, although I'm not a fan of Brosnan."

Georgia scowled. "Nor am I."

"I think he's the best Bond since Connery," said Samuel.

"No way!" said Georgia and Michael simultaneously.

"There's always the new Harry Potter film," suggested Georgia. "If you really want some escapism."

"Oh God, no," said Michael. "I'm not buying into that whole Potter mania."

"Oh, nor am I," insisted Georgia, the blush spreading down her neck.

"We were actually talking about going for something to eat," said Samuel, standing with a groan. "Maybe pizza. Join us if you want."

Michael also stood. "No, you're fine. I'll give one of the boys a call and see if they want to come to the flicks with me. Have fun, you two lovebirds."

As Michael walked away, he glanced back and gave a wave. Georgia was staring after him intently. She looked embarrassed, as if he'd caught her doing something bad. She returned the wave, as did Samuel, before he reached his hand out to Georgia, pulling her to her feet.

Michael was beginning to feel nervous about starting university and leaving home. He hadn't said anything to his parents or Samuel. As far as they were concerned, he was desperate to get away. He was lying on his bed staring at the ceiling, trying to imagine life on campus, when someone knocked lightly on his bedroom door.

"Yeah, come in!" he called. He was expecting to see Samuel or one of his parents, but it was Georgia who opened the door and entered warily, hovering on the far side of the room.

"What's up?" asked Michael, wondering if something had happened to Samuel.

"Samuel has gone to get us some take-out," she said, taking a couple of steps toward the bed.

Michael felt suddenly uncomfortable, which was strange as he liked Georgia, but there was something weird about her this evening.

"That's nice," said Michael, siting up.

Georgia sat on the end of the bed playing with a strand of her long, dark hair.

"When do you go to uni?" she asked.

"In a couple of days."

Suddenly there were tears running down Georgia's cheeks.

"Georgia, what's wrong?" asked Michael. "Have you and Samuel had a row?"

Michael scooted across the bed and put his arm around her quivering shoulders. As soon as he looked into her eyes, he knew he'd made a mistake.

"I'll miss you," she sobbed and pushed her mouth against his.

"Georgia!" Michael shoved her away and leaped up. "What are you doing?"

"I thought you liked me, too!" sobbed Georgia.

A sound on the landing caused them both to look toward the bedroom door.

Samuel stood watching them. His face was ashen. "What the hell . . ." he stammered.

Georgia bolted from the room, pushing past Samuel and clattering down the stairs.

"Get out!" Samuel yelled after her. "It's over! You whore!"

He had obviously seen and heard everything.

Zoe glanced sideways at Michael. He had pulled the car over part way through telling the story and insisted they take a walk across a field. Now he stopped, taking a deep breath. The sound of sheep bleating filled what would have been silence.

"Later that day Georgia took an overdose. No-one believed she meant to kill herself, but she died in hospital two days later. Samuel blamed me for her death and he still does."

"But how can he?" asked Zoe. "You didn't do anything."

"I think he knows that. But his first love still wanted me over him, and I think that's what really irks him. He was devastated by her death, obviously, but in his eyes, I'd even taken away his right to mourn her."

"I can't believe he still blames you after seventeen years. Surely the two of you have discussed it since then. You work together, apart from anything else. You must have spent hours and hours in each other's company."

Michael shrugged and began to walk back toward the car. "It's amazing how you can avoid being on your own with someone if you have to. Up until now, we've managed to be professional at work and civil at family occasions, but something seems to have snapped. If Samuel really is responsible for the health scares and the strikes in Rome, I'm seriously worried about his mental health. I wonder if it has something to do with Lucy."

"How do you mean?" asked Zoe, allowing Michael to hold her hand as she navigated the gate.

"He probably thought I would be devastated when she left me for him, that I would fall apart and he would have to take over the reins. But I didn't. I just kept going. If anything I became more focused at work so that I didn't have to think about the situation. And then I met you, and Lucy ceased to matter that much to me. I think that has tipped him over the edge."

They climbed back into the car and Michael started the engine.

"Anyway, that's the story of Georgia," he said, solemnly. "It affected our whole family for a while. I almost flunked out of university because I felt so guilty."

"But you did the right thing," insisted Zoe. "You rejected an advance from your brother's girlfriend. What options did you have?"

"I just felt bad that I hadn't noticed she was falling for me, or that she was so vulnerable. We all saw her as this happy girl, when inside she was obviously anything but."

"That's still not your fault."

"I know that now. Sadly, my brother obviously hasn't

moved on."

"I'm sorry you had to go through that," said Zoe. "And I'm sorry about having to tell you about Samuel's behaviour. I'd like to spend tonight with you, if that's okay. I don't want you brooding over this on your own."

"You don't need to worry about me. But I'd love you to stay at mine tonight."

"That's settled, then," said Zoe, yawning and sinking into her seat.

"Before you fall asleep," said Michael. "What did you mean about helping to expose Samuel?"

"Let's discuss it over lunch at yours."

"I assumed you'd want to stop for breakfast somewhere," said Michael. "And brunch."

It was good to see him smile.

Zoe must have fallen asleep somewhere just outside London. When she opened her eyes, they were driving down a tree-lined avenue with impressively large detached properties on either side.

"Nearly there," said Michael, turning onto a narrow side road.

"Is this Hampstead?"

"Yes, and my place is just along here," replied Michael as he took a sharp left-hand turn onto a gravel driveway.

Zoe hadn't known what to expect from Michael's home. He'd mentioned it was in Hampstead during one of their chats, but he hadn't said how big it was or how beautiful.

In total contrast to his parents' ultra-modern house, Michael's home was a sprawling Victorian villa, with arched windows and what looked like the green dome of an observatory. It was like something from a fairy tale, where a magician would live.

"You live here?" asked Zoe.

"Yes," replied Michael. "Do you like it?"

"I love it! It's just not what I imagined."

"We Brittons like to surprise," said Michael, parking the car a short distance from the house.

"I just pictured you in some bachelor pad, with lots of chrome and maybe black sheets on the bed," said Zoe with a grin.

"You haven't seen inside yet. Maybe you're right."

She wasn't right about the chrome. The house was a treasure trove of antique furniture, mixed with bespoke modern pieces, expertly crafted to complement the old. Every room had a huge fireplace, and there seemed to be at least three stairways leading up to different sections of the house. The former observatory she had seen from outside was now a library, shelves of books lining the curved walls, with a moving ladder like those in all the best libraries, and there were countless bedrooms, none of which featured a bed with black sheets.

"This is the master bedroom," announced Michael, opening a door on the third floor to reveal a vast room, its centrepiece a huge four-poster bed.

"Shall I leave my bag here?" asked Zoe.

"I'm rather hoping you do," replied Michael.

Zoe dropped her bag next to the bed and followed Michael over to the large, arched window set opposite.

"Wow!" she gasped. The view from the window showed not only the long perfectly mowed lawn, but also the gorgeous Hampstead Heath in all its autumnal glory. The heath was almost an extension of the garden, starting where the lawn ended, just beyond a high wooden fence. Zoe recognised certain locations from her infrequent trips to the heath—the various ponds, Parliament Hill, and beyond an expansive wooded area where she could just make out the Georgian grandeur of Kenwood House.

"This is spectacular," she said. "What a view to wake up to."

"You'll get to experience that for yourself tomorrow."

Zoe felt a surge of excitement at spending another night with Michael, even if the harrowing events of the morning meant passion was put on hold.

"Now," he said, taking her hand and leading her out of the room. "What are you plans regarding Samuel? Please tell me you are not suggesting some kind of honey trap."

"Sort of," admitted Zoe. "I mean it's not rocket science. He obviously wants me to like him to spite you, and in his twisted state of mind, I don't think he will take much convincing that I've fallen for him. I could say yes to that cosy drink and get a full confession out of him, all recorded on my phone, of course."

"You make it sound so simple. But you've missed out the part where he tries to assault you again or sees the phone and goes berserk. Do you really want to be alone with Samuel when he flies into a rage?"

"I won't be on my own," said Zoe. "You'll be hiding in the next room."

Michael pushed open a door on the ground floor and they stepped into a kitchen. It was even bigger than the one at his parents' home. The floor was covered in stone flags, and a ten-foot long wooden island filled the centre. Above it hung every conceivable cooking utensil. Zoe gazed up at them in wonder.

"I don't actually know what any of them are for," said Michael. "I have a private chef who comes in when I'm around and prepares meals for me. Unfortunately, he wasn't expecting me today, so we will have to fend for ourselves."

"I'm sure we can cope between us," said Zoe. "Although, while I love eating food, I'm not the greatest cook."

Michael sighed deeply. "Oh dear. Looks like I need to get myself a new girlfriend."

"I make up for it in other ways," said Zoe, heading over to the towering fridge on the far side of the room. "Let's see what we have to work with."

"I won't let you do it, obviously," said Michael, as Zoe scanned the packed fridge.

"You won't let me make a sandwich?" she asked, pulling out a selection of cheeses and placing them on the island, before returning to forage for more delights.

"No, try and trick Samuel into a confession. This isn't your battle, and I don't want you getting involved."

"I'm already involved," said Zoe, returning to the island with a bowl of home-made potato salad and a large tub of hummus, also home-made by the look of it. Zoe was liking the efforts of Michael's private chef. She loved nothing more than grazing a selection of deli foods.

She found a loaf of crusty bread on the counter, plus a jar of fancy looking chutney in one of the cupboards, and placed these with her other finds.

"Plates?" she asked,

"Zoe, are you listening to me?"

"Yes," said Zoe, opening cupboard after cupboard.

"This one," snapped Michael, pulling open the only cupboard she hadn't looked in to reveal a neat stack of plates in three sizes. Zoe selected two of the biggest and placed them on the island with the food.

"I'm not responding because I'm hoping you'll end up talking yourself into seeing that I'm right," said Zoe. "It was me who saw the call from Dennis Archer, remember, otherwise you'd still think the saboteur was an outsider."

"He could talk his way out of that, say you misread the name, say he managed to track Archer down after speaking to the team in Rome. He'd somehow twist things to make himself look good and you like a paranoid loser."

"Which is why we need that confession," said Zoe,

perching on a stool and surveying the picnic style lunch.

Michael pulled out a drawer on his side of the island and threw a selection of cutlery between them. "Unless you were planning to eat with your hands," he said.

Zoe poked her tongue out at him and spooned a large dollop of hummus onto her plate, then cut a jagged slice of crusty white bread.

"I love how even this conversation—some would call it an argument—isn't stopping you from eating," said Michael, also sitting and helping himself to some bread and cheese.

"I had no breakfast," said Zoe, between mouthfuls.

Zoe loved watching Michael eat. He made even the simple act of biting into a slice of bread and cheese look majestic, sitting so upright, broad shoulders back, no hint of a slouch in his posture.

"What?" he asked, noticing her interest.

"Nothing." Zoe dropped her gaze to her plate. "I was just looking at you and thinking how hot you are."

"Have you ever made love in a four-poster bed before?" asked Michael.

Zoe shook her head, face burning.

"Tonight will be a first, then,"

When Zoe glanced up, his beautiful, dark-blue eyes were boring into her, as if he could bring her to orgasm with a look alone. The way Zoe felt at that moment, the desire that filled her and the shudder of delight his gaze sent through her, she thought maybe he could.

CHAPTER TWELVE

After lunch Michael suggested they go for walk over the heath, and Zoe agreed some exercise would be a good idea after all she'd eaten.

"I haven't been for a run in days," she said.

"It's hard to imagine you actually running."

"Why?"

"You just don't seem the type," said Michael, helping Zoe on with her coat.

"I told you, I run all the time."

"We'll have to go running together one day," said Michael, leading them through the house to a back door that led to the garden.

Zoe pictured herself running, drenched in sweat, red in the face, no make-up, dressed in a baggy sweatshirt and jogging bottoms. "Maybe not for a while," she replied, following Michael into the garden.

A central path led them to a wooden door set in the fence at the end of the lawn, which Michael opened with a key.

"I always wondered who could afford to live in one of the houses with gates leading straight onto the heath," she said

"Now you know." Michael took her hand as they walked down a gentle slope onto a stretch of moorland, scattered with heather and thistles. It was a part of the heath Zoe didn't recognise, but she had never really explored the beautiful place thoroughly.

"Do you think Samuel will have spoken to your father about what happened at the house?" she asked as they ambled along a mud track toward a row of trees.

Michael grunted. "Probably. No doubt he's fabricated his own version of events. I should have got in there first, but I'm too old to be running to Daddy whenever anything goes wrong."

"If you want him to resign, you'll have to speak to your father though, won't you?"

"I said a lot of things back there which I probably can't follow through on. He won't resign. The only chance I have of getting him out of the company is to prove he's been deliberately sabotaging it to make me look bad."

"Well, I have offered my services," Zoe said as they turned onto a wider, more even path running beneath a canopy of trees.

"I wouldn't put you at risk like that."

"Where would be the risk? You'd be in the next room to step in if things went wrong."

"I just don't think he'd be stupid enough to fall for a set-up like that," said Michael, smiling as a huge wolfhound lurched past them, its owner a petite woman who could probably have ridden on her pet's back.

"I don't think he's stupid. But he is obsessed with getting one over on you, so I think he'll believe what he wants to believe, and he's deluded enough to think that I might be interested."

"And how far would you take this charade?" asked Michael, sidestepping a pair of wire-haired terriers whose owners had been left far behind.

"What do you mean?"

"Would you kiss him? Let him touch you again?"

"No!"

"You've seen what he's like. He won't spend an hour making small talk over a glass of fizz, he'll be straight in there, expecting you to show how much you fancy him. Do you find him attractive?"

"Absolutely not. I mean, he's good looking, but he's a creep. I still don't get how Lucy went for him when she had you."

"I guess I have to take some of the blame for that. I wasn't always the most attentive boyfriend. You've seen what I can be like. Sometimes I get lost in work and don't pay the woman I'm with enough attention. I think Lucy convinced herself I was losing interest. Maybe she was right. I mean, look how quickly I got over her. I never felt for her the way I feel for you, and I've only known you a few weeks."

"You were planning to propose to her," Zoe reminded him as they stopped at a point where the path branched off in several directions. After a brief hesitation, Michael took the pathway to their right, which ran alongside a patch of grass where a group of boys and girls were playing a football match, using their school bags as goalposts.

"I know," said Michael. "I guess I can't use the same ring when I propose to you?"

"Don't tease me."

Michael wrapped an arm around her shoulder. "I'm only half-teasing," he said. "I already think you'd make a great wife. I just need to convince you I'd make an incredible husband."

Zoe laughed. "It's a bit early for this conversation." Although she wasn't sure if she'd say no if Michael dropped to his knee here and now and popped the question.

Get a grip! There's a difference between enjoying the adventure and totally losing the plot!

"I know," Michael said. "Don't worry, I'm not there yet! I haven't even seen where you live. You could be a complete slob."

"I am not!"

Their walk took them down another path with woodland on either side. Nearly everyone that passed them seemed to have a dog. Zoe pictured herself sitting by a crackling fire in Michael's house, a beautiful red setter lying at her feet, while Michael poured them both a glass of red wine.

Stop it!

She had to admit, apart from his unhinged brother, Michael was the perfect catch.

"I have a suggestion," said Michael.

"Go on."

"Why don't we drive over to your place, pick up some more clothes, and then you stay at mine for the rest of the week? We can do some work during the day and then spend the evenings getting to know each other even better."

Zoe hesitated. It sounded idyllic, but should she play a little harder to get?

This is the time to enjoy the adventure.

"Okay," she said.

"Great!" Michael stopped and pulled her to him, planting a kiss on her forehead.

"Maybe we could have a coffee and a slice of that cheesecake I saw in the fridge before we drive to mine though," Zoe added.

Zoe had been nervous about inviting Michael into her flat. She couldn't remember how tidy she'd left it, and she didn't want him thinking she actually was a slob. As they pulled up outside, a ticket warden was parading up and down the street, so Michael suggested he drive around the block while she went up and grabbed some clothes.

She sensed something wasn't right as she reached the front door to her flat. She couldn't put her finger on it—something just felt off. As she opened the door, the feeling intensified. She paused in the hallway, listening for any sign of an intruder.

A voice called from the living-room. "Is that you, babe?"

"Doug!" Zoe stormed into the room and found her ex

sitting on the sofa, swigging from a beer bottle.

"What the hell are you doing here?" she demanded.

"I still have a key." Doug's speech slurred. "Did you forget?"

"Yes, I forgot. And having a key doesn't give you the right to use it. How long have you been here?"

Doug shrugged. "About an hour. I took a day off work. I felt too depressed to go in. I really miss you. I thought you'd be working from home."

"I have a new job. Now will you please leave? I'm just getting some stuff and then I'm going back out."

"Going where?" asked Doug, heaving himself from the sofa. Zoe had forgotten how big he was.

"None of your business!" Zoe pointed at the door. "Get out, Doug."

"There's someone else, isn't there?" Doug whined, taking an unsteady step toward her.

"Again, none of your business," Zoe replied. "And I'm warning you now, if you so much as touch me, my knee will be making very hard contact with your groin. Now get out!"

Doug lumbered forward, reaching out for her.

"Come on Zoe!" he groaned.

"Who the hell is this?" asked Michael, suddenly appearing in the doorway. "Get away from her, you oaf!"

Zoe brought her knee up between Doug's legs, and with a loud grunt he dropped to the floor.

"I warned you," she said. "Now go."

Doug looked up at her with glazed eyes, then at Michael, who stood with clenched fists just inside the room.

"Fine," said Doug, using the back of the sofa to pull himself upright. "I can't believe you've already moved on."

Zoe laughed. "Just go, Doug, before you make any more of a fool of yourself."

Doug staggered toward the doorway. For a moment, Zoe

thought Michael was going to block his way, but he stood to one side at the last second allowing Doug to lumber past.

"You really can look after yourself," said Michael.

"I told you," said Zoe, although beneath her cool exterior she did feel shaken.

"I take it that was the ex?"

"I sure can pick them."

"Your taste has definitely improved," said Michael. "Now go pack. If lover boy comes back, I'll take care of him this time. I managed to find a parking space just around the corner, so there's no rush. Nice place, by the way."

"Have a seat. I won't be long."

As she walked to the bedroom, she had a thought. "Damn it!"

"What's wrong?" asked Michael, who was browsing one of her bookshelves.

"Doug still has a key to my flat. I forget to get it back from him."

"Do you want me to call a locksmith? I have just about every tradesperson imaginable in my contacts."

Zoe sighed. "No, it's okay. He's annoying, but I don't think he'll be back. I'll text him later and tell him to post it to me."

Zoe hurried to pack, trying not to let the encounter with Doug spoil the rest of the day. Although she was getting sick of men trying to molest her. Twice in one day! Next time Samuel tried something, she'd give him the same treatment as Doug. She'd only held back earlier because she'd wanted to avoid a confrontation between brothers.

She heard Michael laughing in the living-room.

"What is it?" she asked, wheeling her suitcase from the bedroom.

Michael was still standing by the shelving unit, holding a large hard-back book in his hand.

"The Joy of Sex," he said, eyebrows raised.

"So?" Zoe tried to brazen it out.

Michael held it up. "It's not even a modern version. It's the original from the 1970s. The men all have moustaches!"

"I'm ready to go," said Zoe.

Michael stroked his upper lip. "Do you like men with moustaches?"

"Michael!"

"Slip this in your case," he said, holding out the book.

"Put it back where you found it and let's go. Before I change my mind."

Grinning, Michael put the book back on the shelf.

"It's a collectors' item," mumbled Zoe as she wheeled her case toward the front door.

Behind her, Michael chuckled.

The fire crackled, flames leaping like red and yellow ghosts. Zoe hadn't even realised one could have real fires in London. She'd had no idea there was such a thing as smoke less fuel. Michael jabbed at the pile of wood with a poker and re-joined her on the couch, wrapping an arm around her shoulder.

Zoe leaned her head on his shoulder and stared out of the French windows at the dusk-filled garden.

"We could be in the middle of the countryside," she said. "It's so peaceful here."

"It's the perfect home to return to after a day at work," said Michael. "I enjoy all the excitement that comes from heading up a company, but I also like to escape from it, too."

Zoe stared into Michael's beautiful eyes, which glimmered and danced in the reflected firelight. He stared back wordlessly, then leaned forward and kissed her mouth.

A loud clanging chime broke the spell.

"What on Earth is that?" asked Zoe.

"It's the doorbell," said Michael. "I like to keep things

authentic."

"Authentic if you're the Addams family," Zoe said with a laugh, but Michael looked perturbed.

"I don't get unexpected guests," he said, standing.

Zoe waited for him to return. A few minutes later she heard his voice growing closer, along with the voice of a woman.

"Lucy," she whispered.

Michael looked flustered when he returned to the living room, Lucy following close behind. Her face was blotchy and pale, her eyes bloodshot and puffy.

"Is everything okay?" asked Zoe, trying not to betray how irritated she was by the interruption.

"I've left Samuel," said Lucy. "I'm on the way to my flat. It's not far from here, but I wanted to see Michael first, to let him know what's been going on. He insisted I say anything I had to say in front of you."

"Really?" asked Zoe, feeling uncomfortable.

"I don't want to be having secret conversations with my ex while you're here with me," said Michael. He turned to Lucy, his jaw flexing in evident anger. "Well, what did you want to tell me?"

"I would have phoned," said Lucy, looking from Michael to Zoe. "But my mobile needs charging and I didn't want to leave it."

You wanted to see Michael, you mean.

"Go on," said Michael. He made no indication that Lucy should sit, and she remained standing just inside the room.

Lucy took a deep breath before speaking. "He's the one behind the health scares in LA and London and the strike in Rome," she said. "He's engineering disasters in the hope that you will mess up and he can persuade your father that you should step down and he should become CEO."

Michael grunted. "We'd worked that much out," he said.

"He admitted it to me on the way back from Cornwall," continued Lucy. "We left not long after you. We weren't really in the country-break mood after what happened. He said he wanted to destroy you. I told him I thought his behaviour was completely outrageous, and he lost it. Told me I meant nothing to him, that he'd only pretended to care about me to get one over on you. Everything he does is about getting even with you. I can't believe I've been so stupid."

Lucy sobbed, covering her face with her hands. Zoe was tempted to hug her, but Michael's stern demeanour kept her rooted to the couch.

"Where is he now?" he asked.

"At his flat, I assume," she said between sobs. "I went back with him just to grab some of my belongings and then I caught a cab here. I wanted you to know what was going on. I don't want to be a part of it. I should never have left you for him."

"I'm glad you did," said Michael. "I'm much happier now."

Even Zoe winced at this. Lucy was already broken—he didn't need to kick her while she was down.

"I'm sorry for interrupting your evening," said Lucy, wiping tears from her face. "I just wanted to tell you as soon as possible."

"Thank you," said Michael, gesturing that Lucy should head back toward the front door.

"Maybe Lucy would like a brandy or something," Zoe offered. She couldn't help but feel sorry for the other woman, whatever her true intentions had been in coming to Michael's house.

"No, it's fine," said Lucy. "I should go."

Michael followed Lucy out of the room, but Zoe could tell he wasn't being polite—he was escorting her out, making sure she left.

Zoe stared into the fire, trying to settle on one emotion. She felt sympathy for Lucy. Although she deserved to be treated harshly after what she had done to Michael, did even she deserve such a cold reception when she had been trying to do the right thing? But she also felt angry at the idea that Lucy had come to Michael's in the hope that their relationship could be rekindled.

Suddenly Zoe knew that she didn't want anyone coming between her and Michael, that she would fight for him tooth and nail if she had to.

CHAPTER THIRTEEN

Waking next to Michael was still a wonderful novelty—feeling his warm body pressed to her back, his arm draped protectively across her chest, his face resting against her shoulder. And she loved the morning smell of him. It was the aroma of a man, slightly musky but clean and sensual. Zoe lay in silence, not wanting to burst the idyllic morning bubble.

From the bed she could see the spectacular view of the heath through the huge arched window. Despite it being almost November, the sky was clear blue, and the golden autumnal light filled the room.

She rolled over to face Michael, who stirred as she moved. She stared at his face. His beautiful eyes were still closed, long dark lashes flickering slightly as he began to wake. She wanted to kiss his full, sensual lips as they quivered with each out-breath. This was the view she wanted to wake up to every morning. She didn't care if it was here in this stunning house, in a luxury LA hotel suite or in her small flat in Islington—if Michael's face was the first thing she saw after waking, she'd be happy.

Michael half-opened his eyes, as if to protect her from their full brilliance.

"Morning," he murmured, stroking a hand down her side, making her tingle just as he had during their foreplay the previous night.

"Morning," she responded, wanting to make love again, while they were both still drowsy.

"What time is it?" asked Michael, slowly sitting up and

stretching.

"Seven," said Zoe, glancing at the digital clock next to the bed.

"Damn! I have a video conference call at eight with the hotel manager in Rome. I need to shower. Do you want coffee?"

"Please," said Zoe, trying to hide her disappointment that Michael was about to leave their loving cocoon.

He leaned down and kissed her on the forehead, before throwing back the bedclothes and heading to the en suite bathroom. Zoe admired his naked body as he walked across the bedroom, quivering at the memory of the two of them writhing in ecstasy the night before.

Zoe also threw back the quilt and followed Michael into the bathroom. He was already under the shower, squeezing blue gel into his hand, so Zoe stepped under the warm jets of water, wrapping her arms around him.

"Fancy multi-tasking?" she asked.

Michael laughed and began to massage the shower gel into her shoulders.

"I need to be professional," he insisted.

Zoe slipped a hand down to his crotch, feeling his growing hardness. His hands slid from her shoulders to her breasts. She groaned and pushed against him. The contradiction of his hardness and the slippery sensation created by the water and shower gel was unusually pleasant, so she shifted her hips from side to side, relishing the feel of his soapy member rubbing against her.

Michael placed a hand on the back of her head and kissed her.

"I really don't have time," he said. "I need to look like a CEO, plus I have to drink at least two mugs of coffee before I can speak to anyone."

Zoe felt rejected, but tried not to show it.

"No problem." She stepped away from him and then out

of the shower. "Why don't I go and make us some coffee, save you some time?"

"Thank you," said Michael, continuing to wash.

As Zoe pulled on a bathrobe which was hung on the back of the door, she took a final longing glance at Michael's naked body. To think she had once fantasised about seeing him in this aroused state, and now it was a reality.

Even if he doesn't have time to make love in the morning.

Zoe scolded herself for feeling hurt, but she couldn't help but wonder how many times Lucy had experienced the same sense of rejection when Michael's work had come first. Was that why she'd gone to Samuel?

As she padded across the bedroom, Michael's mobile phone buzzed on his bedside table. She glanced down and saw the name of the caller. Samuel. She hesitated, checked the shower water was still flowing, then picked up the phone and accepted the call.

"Hello," she said, voice stern.

There was a pause at the other end of the call. "Zoe?"

"Who else would it be?"

"With my brother, you never know."

Zoe listened again for the sound of shower water, hoping it would drown out her voice.

"Michael's in the shower," she said. "But I was hoping I'd get a chance to talk to you."

"Really?" Samuel sounded genuinely surprised.

"Yes," continued Zoe, her heart pounding. "Lucy was here last night, and I'm worried that there might still be feelings between her and Michael."

"What's that got to do with me?"

"I just wanted to talk to someone that knew them both," said Zoe. "Work out whether I need to be worried. Plus it would be good to spend some time with you, if you're still interested."

Zoe felt sick, panicking now that the words were out of her

mouth.

"Seriously?" asked Samuel. "I thought you hated me."

"Not at all, Samuel. You just took me by surprise before."

"I can be a little full on sometimes."

"At least people know where they stand with you. Look, I have to go, Michael will be out of the shower soon. Can you meet me at my flat in about two hours?"

"I have work to do," protested Samuel. "And I do actually need to speak to Michael."

"Well, I'll be there," said Zoe. "And I'll get Michael to phone you back."

She ended the call.

Please God, don't let him tell Michael what I've just said.

Zoe was wracked with guilt as she headed to her flat half an hour later. She had told Michael that she'd forgotten the charger for her laptop, and he'd been too preoccupied with setting up his computer for a video conference call to question her in-depth.

As she sat in the back of the cab, she began to panic again. What was she doing, playing games with a man like Samuel? She was now hoping he wouldn't turn up. Surely even in his unstable state of mind he would suspect something. He couldn't seriously believe she would be interested in him or his opinion, after what had happened in Cornwall. But part of her thought he would show. His ego was so out of control, he actually might believe she was attracted to him, or at least that she'd value his input into her relationship with Michael. She'd used both scenarios as bait and would see which one, if either, he took.

Her flat, once so familiar and safe, felt strange today, as if she were a trespasser—maybe because what she was doing was so out of character and because no-one knew she was doing it apart from her and Samuel.

She started to make coffee, then decided she'd had enough

and poured herself a glass of water instead. Her mouth felt dry.

He won't come.

She wandered to the window. A car was pulling up outside. Someone climbed out of the back. Samuel. Zoe clutched her chest, as if to stop her pounding heart breaking free.

What have I done?

Samuel said something to the driver, and the car moved away. At that moment he glanced up and saw Zoe looking down at him. She resisted the urge to jump back out of his view and instead smiled and waved. Feeling sick, she went to her front door and pressed the intercom button.

"Come up," she said, buzzing him in.

A wave of dizziness swept over her and she leaned against the door for a moment, leaping back at the sudden sound of Samuel knocking from the other side.

Why did I do this!

Zoe took a deep breath and opened the door.

"Hi," she greeted Samuel, who was dressed in one of his trademark suits, ready for a day in the office.

"Good morning," said Samuel, who seemed less cocky than usual.

"Come in." Zoe stepped to one side and gestured toward the sofa. "Would you like coffee?"

"Sure."

As she busied herself in the kitchen, Zoe took her mobile phone from the pocket of her jeans and activated the voice notes app. She slipped the phone into a small pocket in the front of her t-shirt. She'd need to be careful not to move around too much, or the rustling would mask any conversation.

She glanced over her shoulder. Samuel was browsing the bookshelves. How long would it be before he discovered The Joy of Sex?

"Here you go." Zoe handed Samuel his coffee. "Milk and

one sugar, that's right isn't it? I remember from Cornwall."

"Well done." Samuel accepted the mug.

They both sat on the sofa, Zoe desperately trying to act calm, while inside she was a confused mix of emotions.

"So, what is it you wanted to see me about so urgently? I almost didn't come, but curiosity got the better of me. Why the sudden change of heart?"

"Like I said, I would value your opinion on Michael and Lucy. Do you think there's still something between them?"

Samuel shrugged. "She didn't mention him much while we were together. But then we were busy having amazing sex most of the time, so it would have been strange if she'd mentioned my brother."

Zoe coughed nervously. "Do you know why she was unhappy with Michael?"

"Who says she was unhappy with him?" asked Samuel, fixing her with his icy grey gaze.

"She left him for you."

"Maybe that had more to do with how much she wanted me," said Samuel, placing his mug on the coffee table and shifting closer to Zoe. "Is that why I'm here now?"

"What?" Coffee slopped over the rim of Zoe's mug due to how much her hand was shaking.

"You didn't invite me here to talk about Michael, did you? You want me, right?"

Say something!

Samuel leaned in for a kiss, and Zoe leaped to her feet, spilling more coffee.

"No!" she exclaimed.

Samuel scowled. "What is this?" he demanded.

"I just wanted to talk," she insisted, placing the now half-empty mug on the table before any more coffee was spilled.

Samuel stood, too and his stance was aggressive.

"Zoe, what the hell is going on?"

"Nothing. I just wanted your advice."

"That's crap, and you know it. I'm the last person you'd come to for advice. If you didn't get me here for sex, why did you set this up?"

"Oh my God!" shrieked Zoe. "You are so arrogant! Why would I want to have sex with you when I have Michael?" *This isn't going to plan!*

"Why, then?" demanded Samuel.

As Zoe floundered for a response, Samuel reached out toward her. For a second, she though he was planning to grab her breast, but instead his hand reached into the pocket of her shirt and pulled out the phone.

"Seriously? You're recording me?"

He deactivated the voice note app and threw the phone onto the floor.

"Samuel, please," Zoe backed away from him, hands held up defensively.

"What were you hoping for?" asked Samuel. "A full confession? Did you seriously think I'd just spill everything? Oh yes, Zoe, I arranged to have the cockroaches slipped into those meals and I engineered the strikes in Rome."

"You did though, didn't you?"

"You know I did," said Samuel. "And you know why. I assume Michael told you about killing my first girlfriend."

"He didn't kill her, Samuel. She committed suicide."

"Because of him!" yelled Samuel, raising his fist as if Michael was in front of him.

Zoe flinched and almost fell as she stumbled backward. "So, all these years later, you've been trying to get your revenge by deliberately sabotaging the family business, to make it look like he's not in control?" she demanded, her voice shaking.

"Don't you think he deserves it?" raged Samuel. "Why should he be CEO? Why should he have the beautiful girlfriend? Why should he be living this charmed life when he destroyed mine?"

"You seem to be doing okay."

Samuel laughed humourlessly. "Yeah, for a few years the penthouse apartment and a string of gorgeous women seemed like the answer, but then I saw him with Lucy, all loved up and happy, and I felt so angry. It brought it all back and I hated him with a renewed passion."

"So you weren't really interested in Lucy," said Zoe. "You just didn't want Michael to have her."

"Exactly," said Samuel. "And he's not going to have you, either. At least, he won't want you by the time I'm done."

Samuel suddenly lunged at her.

Zoe screamed and pushed him away, running for the bedroom, hoping to barricade herself in there until one of the neighbours called the police. But Samuel grabbed her by the hair and pulled her toward him.

"No!" she screamed.

"Get away from her, you bastard!"

Thank God!

Michael crossed the room in two strides and punched Samuel on the jaw, sending his brother flying backward. He landed in a heap, head just missing the edge of the coffee table.

"Michael, I'm sorry," sobbed Zoe. "I was trying to help."

Michael looked from his felled brother to her, and his face didn't soften any.

"Good job you left your front door on the latch," he said. "Did you know I'd be coming to rescue you from this mess?"

"No," said Zoe, trying to control her crying. "I left it open in case I needed to make a quick exit."

Samuel was clambering to his feet, fists clenched, but before he could swing a punch, Michael hit him again, and this time blood sprayed from the other man's nose as he toppled back onto the floor.

"Just be glad that Samuel is such a vengeful bastard," said Michael, face contorted with rage. "He sent me a text with a picture of your front door, letting me know you'd invited him over. He thought he was rubbing my nose in it, another girlfriend betraying me for him."

Samuel groaned and sat up, blood pouring down his face.

"I wouldn't do that," said Zoe. "I love you."

"I know you wouldn't," said Michael, his voice finally less angry. "I guessed what you were up to, and I knew how it would end. Even Samuel isn't that stupid."

Samuel spat blood onto the carpet. He wasn't attempting to stand again.

"Samuel," said Michael, staring down at his brother. "If you want to be the boss that badly, have the job. I'll speak to Father today and tell him I'm standing down."

"What?" Samuel seemed genuinely confused.

"I mean it. I don't need the stress. I want to focus on the important things, like spending time with the woman I love. I don't even need the money. I can sell the house and live off the proceeds for the rest of my life."

"You wouldn't just give in like that," said Samuel.

Michael raised his hands in a gesture of surrender. "It's all yours," he said. "You don't have to cause any more health scares or strikes, just take it, and I hope it makes you happy. Now get out!"

Samuel pulled himself upright using the edge of the coffee table. He hesitated for a moment, as if expecting Michael to deliver a punchline, admit he had no intention of handing over the CEO role to him, but Michael remained silent.

"Go!" snapped Zoe and with a final glare in her direction, Samuel left.

For a few moments after Samuel's departure, neither of them spoke. Finally Zoe broke the silence.

"Did you mean what you said" she asked.

"Which bit?" asked Michael, walking to the window and gazing into the distance.

"About stepping down as CEO?"

"Well, I'm assuming you didn't get anything recorded on your phone that we can use against him." Michael glanced at her mobile which still lay on the floor.

"No," said Zoe, crossing the room to her desk. "But I did capture the whole thing on here."

She clicked the space bar on her laptop, and a view of her face and the room behind her appeared on the screen.

"I set this up when I first got here," she said. "By the time Samuel arrived, the screen was in sleep mode, but the camera was still running. The phone was a back-up."

"Are you serious?" asked Michael, crossing the room to stand next to her. He placed a hand on Zoe's shoulder which she found comforting after his earlier anger.

"Yes, it's all here," she said, scrolling back through the footage. "So if you want to change your mind about handing him the company, I think we have everything we need to have him fired."

Chapter Fourteen

"You're a better person than me," said Zoe, accepting the brandy Michael was offering her.

It had been two days since the confrontation with Samuel and they had managed to enjoy some time together in Hampstead while Michael pondered what to do. They were sitting in one of his numerous living rooms now, a fire roaring in the grate, shadows dancing on the walls.

Michael sat next to her on the Chesterfield sofa and clinked his own brandy glass against hers. "Samuel knows I have enough evidence to hang him, so I think he'll behave from now on. If I showed my father that footage, it would devastate him, plus, much as I hate Samuel right now, if I took his job away from him I think it might tip him over the edge. And he's already standing pretty close. I've suggested he take a couple of months sabbatical, but until after a couple of weeks."

"Why not for a couple of weeks?" asked Zoe, snuggling closer to him.

"Because I want to take you away somewhere nice."

"I don't need to go anywhere. I'm happy here."

Michael raised his eyebrows and stared at her. "You'd rather stay here than go somewhere hot and exotic?"

Zoe took a sip of brandy. "Also, I can't go anywhere yet. I have a job interview next week."

"What?" Michael looked taken aback. "You already have a job."

Zoe smiled. "I think we both know you don't need a full-time personal PR," she said. "I appreciate you helping me out, but if this relationship is going to work, I need to have some independence."

"Fair enough."

Zoe hesitated before asking the next question. "Michael, what about Lucy?"

A shadow passed across Michael's face. "What about her?"

"Well, she's single now and she obviously still has feelings for you. According to Samuel, it was seeing you two so in love that sparked his revenge attempts. Do you seriously not feel anything for her?"

Michael stayed quiet for a while, staring into his brandy as he swirled it round the glass.

"Of course I feel something for her," he said finally. "And, despite what I said, I hated seeing her with him. Not because I was jealous, but because I didn't like seeing someone I had cared so much for being used like that. Who knows, if things were different, maybe I would try again with her, but there's another woman in my life now and I'm totally in love with her, so Lucy has well and truly missed the boat."

"You like the boat metaphor, don't you," said Zoe. "You invited me into your boat when we first met."

"Are you glad you came on board?"

"Oh yes," said Zoe, leaning in for a kiss. "I love you, Michael Britton."

"And I love you, too," said Michael, pressing his lips to hers.

YOU MAY ALSO ENJOY THE FOLLOWING FROM EXTASY BOOKS INC:

Meant To Be
Gen Ryan

Excerpt

With a coffee in one hand and my cell phone in the other, I navigated through the busy streets of downtown Boston. It was my first week here, and I was solo. No boyfriend. No friends. Just me in the big city. Starting fresh.

The crisp air gave way to cooler weather and Halloween was just around the corner. I was a sucker for candy and cute little ones in costumes. A few storefronts were decorated for Halloween, pumpkins and skeletons lining their windows and stairs. I loved fall in New England.

Some days I was lonely. But that was okay. I had a brand-new job at the prestigious literary company, Ink and Pen. I was riding high, not letting anything from my past interfere with my accomplishments.

"What the hell!" I raised my head as my coffee flew from my hands and spilt all over my nicely pressed white shirt. Of course, the cup of hot, delicious goodness hit the ground, and it splattered all over my beige heels.

I danced in place as the heat of the coffee seeped into my

toes and against my chest.

"I'm so sorry. Seems we both were distracted." A man well over six feet tall stood in front of me. His jeans and plain shirt were unscathed from the coffee disaster that had just happened. Which made sense, considering he looked like he'd been plunked right from the heavens. He was a cross between a Greek god and an Abercrombie model. Naturally, the universe would be kind to him.

"It's fine." I sighed and pulled my shirt away from my skin. Why I'd decided to be cute and wear a patterned bra was beyond me.

"Here." The man took off his shirt, revealing a black tank top underneath. And tattoos. Lots and lots of tattoos.

I found it hard not to gawp—okay, well, stare—at the ink that peppered his mocha skin. There were words, a few things that resembled faces, and things I couldn't decipher. I smiled at a small jack-o'-lantern woven between some words about seizing the day. I love Halloween. I usually wasn't a fan of tattoos, but this perfect stranger was a piece of art. Someone worthy of being gawked at. Which I was doing.

Focus.

"No! Please. It's fine. I'll just grab another shirt." My phoned buzzed, reminding me I had to be at Ink and Pen in a half hour to fill out new hire paperwork.

"I have lots at my office. Take it. Don't want people ogling your flower-patterned bra, do you?" He winked and held out his shirt.

Who was I to deny this perfect gentleman his chivalrous act? Plus, I liked admiring his arms. I shrugged.

"Thank you." I tugged the shirt over my body. It was way too big, but it did the trick. I caught a whiff of his cologne and resisted the urge to bring it to my nose and sniff it. That would officially make me creepy.

"Better tell your boyfriend what happened when you go home in another man's shirt," the stranger added.

"No boyfriend." I laughed as I caught a glimpse of my

reflection in the store window. I resembled a child wearing an oversized sleep shirt. All I needed was pigtails, and it'd complete the ensemble.

"Well, in that case, I'm Chase." We shook hands. "Can I replace that coffee? There's a shop around the corner. And our current attire would fit right in."

We both snorted at the craziness of our appearances.

"I'd love to, but I have a meeting in a half hour. Rain check?" Riffling through my purse, I took out a wet wipe and tried my best to salvage my shoes. Thank God it was just paperwork and not my official first day. I was working closely with the head of the company and wanted to make a good first impression. Having coffee-stained shoes and wearing the shirt of a man I'd just met wasn't what I had in mind.

"How about dinner, tonight?"

"Oh, um . . ." My phone buzzed again. Dammit. I was barely going to make it.

"Here, put in your number." Chase handed me his cell, and I entered it. "Perfect. I'll give you a call, and we can set something up. Willow. That's a beautiful name for a beautiful girl."

"Flattery will get you everywhere, Chase. But I have to go. Pleasure to run into you. And thanks for your shirt."

"Anytime you need a shirt. Some pants. I'm your guy." He pointed his thumbs at himself.

Cheesy. But adorable. "Noted! Take care!" I smiled and waved as I walked away.

When I knew I was out of his sight, I brought his shirt closer to my face and took in a deep breath.

This fumbled encounter might turn into something. Or not. But either way, Boston was seeming to be exactly what I needed.

About the Author

M.S. Batham lives in a leafy district of London, England and loves nothing more than curling up with a glass of wine and a good book. Inspiration comes from the nearby Hampstead Heath, where the author can be found walking in all weathers, and from the myriad of exciting people and places that London has to offer.

www.ingramcontent.com/pod-product-compliance
Lightning Source LLC
LaVergne TN
LVHW020634100826
845148LV00012B/2183

* 9 7 8 1 4 8 7 4 3 1 2 4 2 *